ANGUS
FOLK
TALES

The
History
Press

First published 2021

The History Press
The Mill, Brimscombe Port
Stroud, Gloucestershire, GL5 2QG
www.thehistorypress.co.uk

British Library Cataloguing in Publication Data.
A catalogue record for this book is available from the British Library.

ISBN 978 0 7509 9677 8

Typesetting and origination by Typo•glyphix, Burton-on-Trent
Printed and bound in Great Britain by TJ Books Limited, Padstow

CONTENTS

FOREWORD

A landscape without names is an inhuman space. Place names can be formal – given authority by legal document, map or signpost – or informal: 'where the burn floods', or 'the gate by the big oak', or 'where we found the injured hare'. Stories, too, can be formal or informal, written or oral. Sometimes a place gets its name from something that happened so long ago that the original event has been forgotten. Yet most inhabited places, whether farm, inn, glen, village or town, will have an ever-changing stock of stories and memories associated with them, for that is how humans make sense of the locations in which they spend their lives.

It is always worth asking what a simple, common phrase actually means. 'Folk tales', to me, are what ordinary people in a particular place use to mythologise both who they are and where they are, and who was there before them. We live by the facts of history and in the realities of the present, but we also need the mysteries and moral lessons that folk tales and legends give us.

I have stayed in Angus longer now than I've stayed anywhere else, and it informs a great deal of what I write. When I first looked into Erin Farley's collection of rich and varied Angus tales, I had just finished writing a new novel. As I read on, I came across wolves, a banshee, a hermit, a minister with a secret life, whisky-smuggling, wild weather in the glens, and all manner of interactions – some cruel, some kindly – between the powerful and the poor of this land. What struck me was that these very elements were in my novel, yet there they had taken quite different forms. It was as if I had been at the same well from which the tales in this book are drawn, but in a different season.

Maybe that is why, when you read them, you may feel a sense of ownership not only of the stories you may already know, but also of some you don't. And that may be because you recognise a place, or a place name, or a family name, which locates a story, however weird or scary or incredible it is, in familiar territory. This can be both unsettling and reassuring, but it is one of the things that helps to make these tales, some of which are very old indeed, belong to all the folk of Angus today, and to people further afield too. They speak of where we are, and of where we have come from. And, far into the future, people will still tell them and read them, and add tales of our times too, in order to understand who and where *they* are.

James Robertson
Newtyle, March 2021

Acknowledgements

Thank you to my mother, Rowena Smith, for everything – but especially for illustrating these tales so vividly.

And thanks to her sister, my aunt Fiona Brooks, for being a witch.

Thank you to James Robertson for writing such an insightful foreword to this book. I am also grateful for support, local knowledge and helpful comments from Jim Farley, Ella Leith and Scott Gardiner at various stages of writing.

I have been lucky to be supported and encouraged by communities of excellent Scottish storytellers from all airts and pairts – thanks in particular to Tom Muir and everyone else in the Orkney Storytelling Festival team, and to the ever warm and wonderful Blether Taygether group in Dundee. And to Donald Smith, for his enthusiasm for this volume and all he does for the art of storytelling.

My biggest debt is to storytellers and collectors past and present, thanks to whom these tales have lived long enough for us to learn them. The work of James Cargill Guthrie, D.H. Edwards, Andrew Jervise, Alexander Lowson, Duncan Fraser, Betsy Whyte, Sheila Stewart, Jean Rodger, and Maurice Fleming – among many, many others – has been instrumental in continuing the Angus storytelling tradition in spoken and written form. Thank you also to staff past and present at Angus Archives, Dundee Libraries, and the School of Scottish Studies Archives, for helping to look after stories on everyone's behalf.

INTRODUCTION

Angus (or Forfarshire, as it was officially named after the principal town until 1928) is a small county in the centre of Scotland's east coast. On the north-west side of the county, five glens – Glenisla, Glen Prosen, Glen Clova, Glen Esk and Glen Lethnot – lead up towards the Grampian Mountains. In the middle of Angus, the rich agricultural land of Strathmore has been farmed for countless generations. In the south, across the rolling Sidlaw hills, is the city of Dundee, which grew from a tiny walled medieval town into a Victorian industrial power-house. Following the eastern coastline north takes you from the still-busy docks at Dundee past tiny fishing villages, dramatic sandstone cliffs and white sandy beaches, up to the port of Montrose and its wide river basin.

The folklore of Angus is shaped by landscape, people and history. Although we know little of the Pictish people themselves, the intricately carved stones and underground souterrains they left are central to Angus's folklore, speaking to later generations of kelpies, dragons and fairy chambers. More recent history weaves in and out of legend too. The Jacobite uprisings and their aftermath affected a great many of the people of Angus, both the local nobility and the ordinary crofters in the glens, and so these too have left a strong echo in local folklore.

Gaelic was the main language of the glens, particularly the 'top' of the glens, until at least the late seventeenth century (and there were still native Gaelic speakers living there into the nineteenth). Some of the people in these stories – like the Glenisla hero McComie Mhor – would have spoken Gaelic as their first language. The rest of the characters here – and most of these who

shared these stories around the farms and towns of Angus –
would generally have spoken Scots. Although this book overall
is in English, there are some things which don't translate, and
you will find some of the characters speak Scots because they
quite rightly refuse to speak anything else.

Stories live alongside music, song and poetry as part of everyday culture. The hard work of agriculture was, and remains, a
way of life in Angus, as was the making of cloth in the towns
and cities. Many a song and story were born and sent into the
world among farm workers in bothies and kitchens, or among
the clack of looms in weaving sheds and jute mills. The Traveller
community, who walked the straths and glens and found work
at many an Angus harvest, kept song and story alive here as they
did in so many parts of Scotland. The rhythms of work and the
land, and the often uneasy relationship with the 'big families'
who own it, are a constant backdrop to these tales.

A powerful sense of history, place and fate runs through the
stories here, but the dramatic and supernatural are at home in
the everyday, and they come with a wry sense of humour. This is
a world where ministers spar with the Devil like a quarrelsome
neighbour, ghosts still think about getting the neeps pulled, and
the way you make porridge might be the only thing standing
between you and your freedom. The folk of the farm toons of
Angus, as David Kerr Cameron wrote in *The Ballad and the
Plough*, had their dour moments but were also often 'droll to the
point of eccentricity'. This, I think, sums it up quite well.

Perhaps the best illustration of the Angus attitude to life
is the story of Forfar Castle. During the Scottish Wars of
Independence, Forfar was a royal seat, and of course this meant
it was subject to constant attack. The castle was occupied by
the English for years, until it was won back for the Scots by
Robert the Bruce in 1308. Tradition says that instead of rebuilding the damaged castle, the people of Forfar dismantled its walls
completely, and refused point blank to raise another one. The

honour of housing royalty was hardly worth the hassle of invading soldiers getting in the way of market day.

I grew up in Edinburgh, which has plenty of its own legends, but visits to family in Angus are the setting for my earliest memories of a sense of stories. Spending holidays with my grandparents on my mum's side in Forfar, I remember visiting Glamis Castle, looking up at the windows and wondering which one might be the secret room, spotting fairy-rings of mushrooms by Restenneth Priory, and the sheer terror that the Meffan Museum's stories of witch-burnings instilled in me. My family on my dad's side were in Dundee, and I have vivid memories of looking for ghosts through the windows of abandoned jute mills there after hearing they might lurk there.

I was clearly a spooky child, but I think this came from a fascination with tradition and the presence of the past rather than being morbid for its own sake. While traditional storytelling never really went away, it has certainly seen a huge revival in interest and attention in Scotland in recent years – exciting times for someone like me to live in. As I started going to storytelling sessions and events, I thought back to these legends of secret rooms and haunted mills, and particularly to the story of Jockie Barefit, which my Aunt Fiona scared me with as a child, and which remains my favourite to tell to this day. I started to wonder if perhaps I did know some stories after all, and if storytelling might be something I could do ... Soon, I began seeking out more stories from these places and telling them at every opportunity, and life brought me to Dundee, where I have been lucky enough to get to know them better as part of my work in the libraries' Local History Centre.

These stories matter. As the way we live in a landscape changes, paths to farms and wells that people walked daily threaten to fade into the hillside, and buildings are torn down and replaced. Many of these changes are very welcome – these tales leave you in no doubt that life was not easy in the past. But stories are supposed to keep going, picking up layers of meaning and carrying the experience of their tellers through the years, to tell us something about where we have come from and where we might want to go. Sometimes, they stop and rest on a page for a while. I hope that this book brings readers a new perspective on some of the places they know, and brings these stories to new voices and new ways of telling.

1

LEGENDS OF THE GLENS

The Angus glens are a striking Highland landscape. In days past, there were small farming communities through the glens, and shepherds wandered the higher ground with their flocks. And the glens had plenty of dangers. Wolves roamed the hills, and the narrow, exposed roads brought threats from both weather and raiders. And in the dark nights, the glens were stalked by spirits tied to past sorrows. Glen Lethnot in particular was known for being a superstitious and haunted place long after the Kirk would have liked it to be.

THE TWINS OF EDZELL

In the days of King Robert the Bruce, the country of Angus was thick with forests. On the edge of one of those forests was Edzell Castle, the stronghold which guarded the foot of Glenesk. Around the castle walls, there was a small village. Among the people there was a young couple – a man who worked in the castle's fields and his wife, a Traveller woman who had fallen in love as her family passed through the area and had settled there with him. She was a bit of a mystery to the folk there, and a lot of them believed she had some magic about her. People would sometimes ask her to tell their fortunes – who will I marry, what will the harvest be like, will my son return from his travels? She would think deeply for a while and give them answers, and the things she said usually came to pass.

The couple were expecting their first child when the man fell ill and died, and his wife had to prepare to raise her child alone. But it turned out she had not one child to raise, but two. She gave birth to twin boys, who each had a striking birthmark – one had a bright red spot on his left cheek, and the other had a similar mark on his forehead. She immediately fell in love with her two babies, and she made their living by making pegs and baskets and selling them around the houses of Edzell, and by telling the fortunes of those who asked her. But along with the admiration for her gift came a bit of suspicion. Those who did not trust her power feared it.

As the boys got older, it was clear that they were both deaf, and neither heard nor spoke. But the woman and her sons learned to sign to each other with their hands, and all was well. The twins thrived. They both grew strong and fast, and among the lads of the village they were the fastest runners, the highest jumpers, the strongest wrestlers – and they were by far the best hunters. By their teens they could hunt and fish as well as any of the laird's men. The family home was well stocked with trout from the river, and they could always get meat from deer or even the wild boars which roamed the forest, for they could trap even these ferocious animals. There were rumours that they had even brought home the skins of wolves to warm themselves in winter.

The other young men of Edzell began to shun the twins. They were jealous of their skills, and it turned into hatred. They were also a little bit more afraid of their mother's powers than they would admit. But the two of them were happy enough in each other's company. Their mother worried, though, that they would one day face worse than loneliness because of who they were. She knew what it was like to feel everyone look at her as she passed through the village, and she feared that her sons, being deaf, would suffer even more for their difference. She thought it was best if people feared her and her sons, because there was at least power in that. So she laughed to herself when she heard folk talk about the magic powers her family was supposed to have, and she said nothing to put their minds at rest. Even Sir Crawford of Edzell Castle was wary of them. Sometimes he would give the family a little money, saying it was because he was sorry for their father's death, but really, he wanted to keep on the right side of them.

One day, the wolves in the Forest of Menmuir ventured out, and ripped a flock of the king's sheep to shreds. All the lords of Angus were called to a great wolf-hunt to seek the culprits, and they were told to bring their best hunters with them. So the word was sent round that Sir Crawford wanted hunters to meet at the castle gates before the hunt, and the young men of Edzell duly gathered there, all carrying fine spears and javelins. As the band of hunters prepared to leave, up walked the twins. They had no fine weaponry. Each carried a big rough sack over one shoulder, and had a knife tucked into their belt. This was all they brought. The other young men scoffed and giggled at the sight of them, and all stared openly at the birthmarks on their faces. But Crawford knew there was more to them than met the eye.

As the hunting party made their way into the glen and along the north spur of the White Caterthun Hill, there they sighted a pack of wolves prowling in the trees. Crawford directed six men to block their escape routes, then guided the rest of the hunting party to back the wolves into a clearing where they would be trapped. Crawford's hunting dogs set about them, but the wolves fought well, sinking their yellow teeth into the dogs' throats, moving too fast to be caught by the party's spears.

Then the twins crept forward, gesturing that the others should hang back. Their footsteps fell dead silent in the forest. Then they took the sacks from their shoulders and held them open. From each sack flew seven huge hawks. In an instant, each hawk made for a different wolf, gripping talons into their necks until their white fur stained red, pecking at the eyes of the wolves until they hung down on their stalks. The forest echoed with howls. As the blinded, hopeless wolves staggered around, the twins ran forward and slit their throats with their knives. Crawford and his men stood aghast through all this. They had seen nothing like it before.

At the end of the day's wolf hunt, the men of Edzell were the undoubted champions. Some parties caught one or two wolves, while others returned empty-handed, but Crawford's men could hardly move under the weight of the wolf-bodies they carried home.

But even after this success, the twins and their mother were not truly welcomed into the community. Lord Crawford, seeing their power, appointed them hunters-in-chief on his estate. But neither he nor his wife ever tried to extend a hand in friendship, and nor did the other folk in the village.

As time went by, another rumour was added to those of the family's eerie powers. Folk said the twins were doing some unofficial hunting of their own, out of sight of Lord Crawford, selling deer from the estate around the small settlements further up the glen. Crawford had them watched day and night, but it was no easy task to catch such good hunters in the act. They knew immediately when they were being followed.

One night, a windy night in late September when the full moon lit the sky, Crawford held a great ball in Edzell Castle to celebrate the end of the harvest. The lord and lady and their guests gathered inside, and, on the green outside, the servants and farm workers from Crawford's estate held their own dances. The only ones missing were the twins and their mother. In their absence, everyone's minds were on them. What did they get up to, these strange people who would not join them on a night like this? The other estate workers decided to do a bit of spying. They crept into the woods and hid behind trees, surrounding the little cottage where the twins lived with their mother.

After a while, the two young men emerged out of the forest. Between them they held a huge red stag, its antlers spreading like branches. It had been killed by a single arrow to its heart. As they came near to the door of their cottage, their fellow workers rushed from the trees and set upon them. Though either of the twins could easily have fought off three other men, they were far outnumbered. The mob tied their hands and feet together and carried them off to the castle, along with the stag as evidence. They called for Lord Crawford to come out from the midst of the dance, to see what his chief hunters had done. He sent them down to be held in the castle dungeon, awaiting their fate the following morning.

For hunting the lord's deer without his permission, the punishment was death. They were to be hanged from a tall oak tree beside the castle. The crowd who had betrayed them the night before were only too happy to hear that they would finally be rid of the twins. At first light, the hangman set about his grim task, while Lord and Lady Crawford looked out from the castle window.

As their bodies hung in the breeze, the twins' mother came rushing out of the forest. At once, she saw she was too late to save her beloved sons. Standing below the window, she pointed her finger at the Lord and Lady Crawford and howled with unearthly fury.

'By all the demons of hell you will be cursed! Lady Crawford, may you know the pain of seeing your bairn die. And Lord Crawford – may you die the most fearful death any man born of woman ever knew!'

Although Crawford's men made to grab her, the twins' mother slipped from their grasp and darted back into the shadow of the forest. It was the last she was ever seen or heard of in Edzell.

But her words remained in the Crawfords' minds. Before that week was out, both Lady Crawford and her young son were gravely ill. The child died and his grieving mother followed a day or so later, and the two were buried in one grave.

But Lord Crawford lived, and he mourned his wife and child for a year before he began the search for a new bride to carry on his lineage. He got engaged to the daughter of a minor noble from the west, and they made plans for a wedding. As part of the celebrations, he declared they would have a hunting party, the first to go out in Edzell since the twins had died.

On a bright autumn morning, Crawford led his party into the forest. Soon they saw a stag break cover, flashing out from among the trees. Off they went after it. The stag led the hunting party into the glen, towards the White Caterthun Hill, until Crawford realised it had led them to the same clearing where the twins had killed the wolves two years before. He shot an arrow and made his target, and the deer fell to the ground. But the place made him feel uneasy. Before he knew what was happening, two ferocious wolves were upon him. They dragged him from his horse with their teeth, ripping his cloak to shreds and then biting into his flesh. By the time his companions heard his screams, Lord Crawford was unrecognisable. The wolves tore him limb from limb and the forest floor was awash with blood.

The hunting party fled in terror, with no choice but to leave Crawford to his fate. When they told their story later, they said that they would know the wolves again, for one had a bright white spot of fur on its cheek, and the other had the same mark on its forehead.

The old Edzell Castle is now gone, replaced by a more modern building, and the oak tree gone with it. But for centuries after these events, on stormy moonlit nights, the spirits of the twins were seen signing to one another beneath its branches, and the forest would echo with the howls of wolves.

The Crying Banshee of Glenisla

This is one of Stanley Robertson's stories. In fact, the young man who it happened to was Stanley's grandfather.

One autumn, a young Traveller man was making his way alone through Glenisla. Autumn days are beautiful in the glens, but at night, the cold and the winds are a danger. It was a dreich night he found himself out on, and rain was battering down. His feet ached from a long day's walking and his hands were red raw from making the besoms he sold, and the cold and the wet made his hands and feet hurt even more.

He didn't see another soul on the road through Glenisla, just the steep braes looming up on either side of him and the burn running along beside him. There was barely even a bird or a fox for company. He knew some of his family would be camped five or six miles along the glen, but the thought of walking that far was too much. So the man made up his mind that he was going to stop in at the next shelter he came to, whether that meant making up a camp by himself or asking if he could sleep in someone's barn. After a while he caught sight of a wee house that was set a bit back from the road. He hoped there would be a fire on inside and maybe a bite to eat. But when he approached it he saw his luck was out again. It was an old bothy, one of the ones that the unmarried farm workers lived in. But this one had been abandoned for years, and the windows were boarded shut. The farmhouse itself, not far away, was just a pile of rubble.

'Och well,' the man thought to himself. 'I've spent the night in worse places, this'll do me.'

So he went inside the bothy and looked around. There was an old-fashioned fireplace, and he did his best to scrape out the dirt and set a fire going with the driest bits of heather he could find. Soon he was getting warmed up and the room was smoky from the wind blowing back down the chimney. It felt so good to be inside in the warm.

But the old door was swinging to and fro with a creak and a bang, and it was letting a cold draught in that cut through the heat from the fire. He ventured out into the night again and got a big, round stone, so heavy he had to stagger with it, and he heaved that inside and set it against the door to jam it shut. Peace at last. He took out his pipe and dug in his pack for a bite to eat. It was beginning to feel quite cosy in there, and soon he lay down by the fire and drifted off to sleep.

Bang, bang, bang! He woke up to an almighty noise at the bothy door. It was the dead of night, almost pitch dark apart from a bit of light from the embers of the fire. Whatever it was kept battering at the door like it was going to break it down.

The young man lay stock still. The noise was far too loud to be a human knock. Then suddenly it fell dead silent, so quiet he thought there could be no life for miles. And in that silence, a low, mournful howl started to echo through the glen.

'It must be the wind coming doon the lum,' he told himself. 'It's just the wind.'

Then came the *bang, bang, bang* of whatever was crashing against the door. He thought the door was about to come clean off its hinges. And then he realised that the wind couldn't be coming down the lum and crashing against the door at the same time, for those were two different sides of the bothy. His instinct told him he wasn't safe where he was beside the fire, and he crept off towards the other end of the room. The door kept bang, bang, banging away.

For a few minutes, all was quiet. But then, the mournful howl came again, drifting through the night air and sending a chill into his bones that went deeper than the cold. It howled and sobbed, and then the crashing at the door started again. He was absolutely petrified by now, pressed up against the wall as far away from the door as he could get, praying whatever it was wouldn't make it in.

Then – *crash!* Even louder than before, and the door burst open. The big stone he'd put against the door came flying through the air and smashed down into the hearth. It landed just where his head had been minutes before. If he had still been lying by the fire, that would have been the end of him.

The night was silent again. But the young man was not going to hang around and find out what might come next.

He got to his feet and picked up his basket. As he stepped out of the bothy door, he heard the voice moaning and howling, further away now.

'I'd better get away afore it comes back this way,' he said to himself, and made for the road. And then he saw it. The ghost. It was a huge white shape sweeping across the glen and it was crossing over and over the roof of the bothy. Every time it flew over the roof, the doors and windows shook as if the whole place was about to fall down. He shuddered to think it had been right over his head while he'd been in there.

Now his sore feet were the least of his worries, and he ran down the road and through bushes and streams and ditches towards where his family had said they'd be camping. Whatever would get him away from that bothy the fastest was the route he took. He didn't take a minute's rest until he got there. When he arrived, so relieved to see another living soul, he saw the folk there were all packing up their tents and getting ready to leave again too.

'Oh, you're here,' they said. 'Just as well. We're no biding here, there's a crying banshee in Glenisla tonight.'

They had seen the spectre too, and heard it crying up and down the glen all night. They told him it had been blowing their tents down and howling around the camp. When it had been quiet at the bothy, the banshee had been down at their camp, and when it had been quiet there it had been up crashing and banging at the bothy door. The banshee was a lonely spirit, the ghost of someone who had died without kith or kin. This one was mourning a battle which had been lost in the glen many years before, in which the last of its people had died.

Stanley Robertson said that Glenisla and Glen Clova were always known as bad places to spend the night among the Traveller folk, because they were haunted by many such mournful banshees.

McComie Mhor

High up Glenisla, at a place called Crandart near Forter Castle, there once lived a man named Iain MacThomaidh, the head of the clan MacThomas. As the years went by, the Scots speakers of the glens passed his name down phonetically as McComie. He was known in the area as McComie Mhor, and he was famous for his many adventures across the glens of Angus and Perthshire.

Like his Gaelic name suggests, he was a big man, so big as to be almost a giant, and he always wore a red jacket with silver buttons in the style of the reivers of the glens. McComie was renowned for his strength and bravery, and when the glens held their Highland Games his athletic feats were second to none.

He could pick up gigantic boulders with one hand that no one else could shift with two and hurl them far across the playing field. Near where the source of the Isla springs up, there are two such boulders still known as McComie's Stones, which no one has been able to move in the centuries since he threw them.

McComie had seven sons, and to each of them he passed on his legendary size and strength. But as they grew, he began to suspect his eldest son had not quite inherited the bravery he needed to go with it. He decided to test the boy. One day McComie disguised himself in a big cloak and hood, and he sat awaiting his son not far from their house at Crandart, at a spot where he would be sure to catch him on the way home. He chose a large stone to sit on while he waited, a stone which would become known as McComie's Chair. When he saw his son approaching, he ambushed him, and there followed a long and bloody fight between father and son. They battled each other for hours, and neither could gain the upper hand. Eventually, this satisfied McComie that his son was a match for him, and so he'd be more than a match for anyone else he might cross. So he stepped back from the fray and pulled down his hood to reveal his face. His son's sword fell from his hand in sheer astonishment.

After that, father and son got on very well. The two of them decided to build a lime kiln at Crandart, and they built as big and impressive a kiln as you would expect. But the huge stone they had set aside for the lintel was a challenge even for them. One day they tried all morning to heave it into place, but neither could manage it. They took a break to have dinner, and while they were away, a man named Colin McKenzie passed through the glen. Seeing the stone, he thought the builders could do with a hand, and heaved it into its rightful place. Coming back to see this, McComie was stunned, but very impressed. He took off the jacket he was wearing, his famous one with silver buttons, and gave it to McKenzie as a token of his admiration. Silver buttons were a point of honour for the reivers of the glens, for if you killed a man in battle who wore a jacket of this style, you were honour-bound to take the buttons and use them to make sure that he got a good Christian burial of the kind you would wish for yourself.

There is one more element to McComie's story, perhaps the most intriguing part. McComie would often wander off to a little loch in the glen, the Crooked Loch, and when he arrived there, out of the dark peaty water would swim a mermaid. She would come and sit on the edge of the loch and the two of them talked for hours, swapping stories from the world of humans and that of the mermaids and fairy folk. She was very curious about the ways of the human world. One day she leaped up onto the back of McComie's horse – sitting side-saddle with her tail over to one side – and rode down the glen behind him to see the ways of the folk there for herself. McComie and his mermaid were the speak of the place for weeks.

But since McComie died, and was buried at the Kirkton of Glenisla, his mermaid has never been seen by anybody else. And – stranger still – nor has her lochan. You can walk the length of Glenisla and not catch a glimpse of anything like the wee Crooked Loch in which she lived. But perhaps, one day, she may choose to reveal herself again.

THE LAST WOLF

Wolves were once common in the glens and forests of Scotland, but people always feared them, and they were hunted to the brink of extinction. The time came when there was only one wolf left in Angus, and Glen Lethnot was its home. Although the creature was rarely seen, it did make the occasional foray into the farms to snatch sheep from the flocks. For these crimes, the young laird Robertson of Nathro was determined to have its head.

One summer, a young servant girl was sent from her farm to the mill of Glascorry, near the Caterthun hills, to sift a grinding of corn. She had been given a heavy load, and the work was hard, and the day was hot. Once she had finished her toil at the mill, the girl lay down for a rest in the sunshine before heading back to the farm. She leant back against a tree and sighed. Surely shutting her eyes for just a minute would do no harm. But she drifted off to sleep.

The girl awoke with a start, not knowing how long she had slept. She could feel something heavy dragging down the hem of her shawl at her side. As she looked round to see what it was, she was horrified to see the grey hairy bulk of the last wolf in Angus snoring away beside her.

Trying to move as gently and quietly as she possibly could, she untied the shawl from round her shoulders and gingerly got to her feet, picking up the bowl of corn, and backing away step by step until she thought she had enough distance between her and the creature to give her the advantage. Then she broke into a run and hurried home as fast as she could.

The tale of the wolf quickly overshadowed her late return. When word got to Robertson of Nathro, he sprung into action and set out on its trail, returning to the spot where she had awoken. The wolf was gone, but on the spot lay fragments of the girl's shawl. The wolf had torn it to shreds, and the threads and scraps of fabric led the beast's trail into the hills. Robertson followed them until he caught sight of the wolf, and he trailed it along the Caterthun hillside until the creature was firmly in his sight. With one shot from his gun, the last wolf in Angus was no more.

Robertson returned triumphant. He was so delighted to have finally defeated the wolf that he married the servant girl who had led him to his quarry, so her days of toil were over too.

THE MINISTER'S CURSE

There was once a minister at Kirkton of Glenisla who found himself at the centre of a great scandal. Rumours were flying around that he had seduced one of his parishioners, and that he was the father of her unborn child. He denied it, but his voice was one against a chorus of accusations. The loudest voice that spoke out against him was that of Captain Thomas Ogilvie of Eastmill, and his five sons backed him up. The family at Eastmill, a respectable house on the banks of the Muckleburn, were well thought of in the area, and their word was taken seriously. Eventually, the minister became so tormented that he had no choice but to leave the parish. But he was not going to leave it without having his say.

On his last Sunday in Glenisla, the minister found the congregation had locked the church door against him. So he stood on the step at the manse door and preached to anyone who would listen a sermon of fire and brimstone, horror and revenge. And he preached that the family of Eastmill would have their comeuppance. His sermon ended with the words: 'If these men die the death common to men, God hath not spoken by me!'

Although the minister was gone the next morning, his words echoed in the minds of the Ogilvies of Eastmill over the months to come. By the time the year was out, Thomas's eldest son was overtaken by depression, and he hanged himself in the sheep bucht. The second son, William, decided to escape to sea, but before he set foot on a boat he was crushed to death in an accident at Dundee docks. And as for Thomas himself, his part in the Jacobite uprising caught up with him, and he spent five lonely years imprisoned in Edinburgh Castle. His desperation led him to try to escape, breaking out of his cell one night and trying to clamber down the castle crag. His body was found at the foot of the rocks the next morning.

This left three of Thomas's sons. The eldest living son was also named Thomas, and he became the owner of the house at Eastmill. Another, Patrick, was in the West Indies on army service. And the youngest, Alexander, left Glenisla for Edinburgh, where he married a carter's daughter – somewhat below himself, his father would have said had he lived.

In time, the new Thomas Ogilvie of Eastmill became an eccentric bachelor. These were the days when wearing tartan was prohibited in Scotland, but he insisted on wearing the old-style full plaid, in hodden grey. Everyone was surprised when he announced his engagement to young Katherine Nairn. She was a baronet's daughter, and twenty years younger than him, but she was keen to marry this odd man with an empty bank and a family curse. So Katherine came home to Eastmill, and a little while later Patrick came home from the army, and their cousin Anne arrived for a long visit.

The house on the banks of the burn began to feel very full. Everyone was living on top of one another, especially Katherine and Patrick, who became very close while Thomas was out of the house at work. Rumours began to buzz around Eastmill. Cousin Anne said to Thomas that she had come home one day to hear unmistakable sounds from Patrick's bedroom, when Patrick and Katherine had thought they were alone. But Thomas told Anne she was just a gossip.

In the end, it was lace that was the undoing of things. Katherine had been taking extra money from the household to buy lace to make gifts for Patrick, fancy collars and cuffs in the latest fashions. But her husband was a thrifty man, and would not have this frivolity – really, the waste bothered him more than the infidelity. The three of them ended up in a screaming row in the kitchen.

'I wish I was dead!' Katherine howled at her husband. 'Or that you were!'

Patrick packed his bags after that, and took his collars and cuffs off to find somewhere else to stay. But things were still cold between Thomas and Katherine. They barely spoke a word to one another. Then Thomas began to grow ill. He could barely walk a mile, and his bones ached day and night. He became confined to bed, and not long after that he was dead. The tongues of Glenisla wagged, and it was Katherine they spoke of. Even Anne joined the chorus, saying she'd heard the young woman talk of poisoning her husband to be with his brother. Soon the guards arrived to bring Katherine and Patrick to Forfar jail on a charge of murder. Katherine begged them to take the carriage the long way by the back road, so that the neighbours did not see her shame.

The pair were found guilty, and Patrick was sentenced to hanging for his crimes. He slipped from the noose at the first attempt, but soon the gathered crowds saw him dead. Katherine had been sentenced to the same fate, but hers was delayed – she was pregnant. Nine months after Thomas's death, she gave birth to a baby girl in Forfar jail. While the judges argued over when a suitable new execution date would be, Katherine sneaked a guard's uniform from a laundry pile and slipped away to her freedom.

She was not an Ogilvy by blood, so the curse did not seal her fate. Some say she married again, a richer man, and went to live in Europe. Some say she'd had enough of all that by then, and went into a convent to see out the rest of her days. And others say she did not manage to escape very far after all, and that the rest of her life was spent wearing the rough robes of a hawker, selling odds and ends up and down Glenisla. But the daughter she had left in the cell had Ogilvy blood no matter which brother was the father. She was accidentally smothered by the midwife who'd been charged with her care, when she was only a few days old. And who knows, perhaps it was best for the poor thing that she didn't live to see worse fates.

This left one Ogilvy brother. Alexander, the youngest, was now the owner of Eastmill. It was not a huge estate, but it was something, and he thought he could now do better than a carter's daughter for a wife. When he returned to Glenisla he left his wife behind, and found himself an army officer's daughter to marry instead. Of course, her family wanted a fancy wedding, and where else could this take place but fashionable Edinburgh? Seeing the wedding notice posted, Alexander's first wife made her way to the church where they'd been married years before and got proof of his existing union. As Alexander Ogilvy stood in the Canongate Kirk, instead of his new bride coming down the aisle, he saw the City Guards. They told him he was being banished from Scotland for bigamy. Defeated, he returned to the nearby tenement he had taken a top-floor lodging in and packed his belongings. Alexander turned to whisky to soothe his soul, and he got so horribly drunk that he tripped over his bags and went flying right out of the tiny window. And so the minister's curse was fulfilled, and the Ogilvies of Eastmill were finished.

The Devil in Lethnot

Farmer Black of Wirren was a grumpy old sod. He had many enemies, but the very worst was his neighbour. He could not remember exactly why he hated the man so much, but the farmer was certain he'd done something to deserve it years before. Black's long-suffering wife and their wee son listened to hours of tirades about the man. He never planted his tatties at the right time, he stayed too long in the pub in Edzell on market days, he was in general a sham of a farmer and a terrible excuse for a human being. One Saturday night, Black had himself worked up into such a state that he got the notion into his head to go over and give the man a piece of his mind.

'Och, don't do that,' said his wife. 'You'll just start trouble. Leave it to the morn and see how you feel then.' She had a feeling her husband would not come out on top if it came to blows.

But none of her persuasions were working. Her husband was determined. She decided to try a different tack.

'Who will keep me company tonight if you're off quarrelling?'

'Och, the Devil if he likes!' shouted Black, and stormed out of the door.

It turns out he did like. No sooner had the door closed than up came a big puff of smoke and brimstone in the middle of the living room floor, and there was Auld Clootie, ready for a night of mischief and torment with the mistress of Wirren. But after years with her troublesome husband, she was able for it.

She whispered instructions into her son's ear and slipped him
out of the window at the back of the house. He ran as fast as he
could to the nearby manse at Lethnot. When he returned, he
had Reverend Thomson with him, in full gown, Bible in hand
– and a fair crowd of neighbours dying to catch a glimpse of the
Devil too.

When the Devil saw the Reverend standing in the doorway holding the Holy Book, he just laughed. But he wasn't laughing long. Thomson reached inside his robe and drew out a huge sword. He yelled and launched himself at the fiend. The Devil was so surprised he let out an awful shriek, and fled in the same cloud of smoke and brimstone he'd arrived in. From that day on, there was always a great dent in the floor where the Devil had made his way out.

And the Devil was always one to bear a grudge. Although he never quite had the courage to face Thomson head-on again, he kept a special place in his malicious heart for the manse at Lethnot. When Thomson sat at his desk to write his sermons, his study would be engulfed in darkness, even in the middle of the day. If he lit a candle it would burn weakly. One day, Thomson sat down and knew the Devil was lurking behind him. He reached out for a small scrap of paper and wrote down the first Promise of the Bible on it. He tossed it over his right shoulder, saying, 'Tak that, Satan, it's low water wi ye noo!'

This was enough to send the Devil away for a good long while. And by the time he returned to Lethnot there was a new minister for him to deal with. You see, Thomson was popular with his parishioners, but not so much with the Church. As a Jacobite sympathiser, his prayers for the Rebel Army were cause for suspicion – and besides, there was all this nonsense about fighting the Devil, who had no place in a modern Scotland and wasn't to be encouraged. So the Church sent a new minister named John Row, whose mission was to stamp out all traces of superstition in the newly united parishes of Navar and Lethnot.

Reverend John Row was determined to prove the old beliefs wrong. One superstition that the people of Lethnot all held was the idea that anyone who stepped over a newly made grave would face misfortune before long. So, at the end of one funeral service, John Row closed his Bible and stepped away with a long stride right over the new grave. And just to make his point clear, he stepped back over it and again, a third time.

And then home he went to the manse, and up to his study to write a sermon on the values of sensible thinking. As soon as he crossed the study threshold, Row felt a chill, and he became certain something uncanny was lurking there in the shadows. He called down to his servant to bring up a light and a stick of some kind. The girl grabbed an old straw fork from the garden, lit a candle, and hurried up the stairs.

Holding the candle below the desk, Row saw a large, hairy black cat with eerie glowing amber eyes crouched in the shadows. When it saw the flame, the cat hissed and sprang to life. It bolted between his legs and shot towards the door. The minister gave chase and ran after the cat, staggering down the stairs brandishing the fork. He swung his weapon round to hit the creature and lost his balance, crashing against the wooden railing on the side of the stair. The wood was old, and it gave way under his weight. Row fell to the stone floor below, and his back was broken clean in two.

COBB'S HEUGH

James Black was the miller at Lethnot. He was the brother of Black of Wirren, the grumpy farmer who summoned the Devil, and he took after his brother in temperament. The laird of Lethnot was one of the Lindsay family, and he had a fair temper on him too. The two of them were always at war over something. So when, one month, Black was late with his rent – again – the laird stormed down to the mill and demanded cash.

'It's been a bad year for the crops,' said the miller. 'I cannae pay my rent when nobody pays me. Besides, the place is no fit to be paid for. The roof's been leaking for months.'

'I can't pay for repairs when I get no income from rent,' said the laird. 'I don't do this out of the goodness of my heart.'

'Aye, there's little enough of that to go round,' said Black, 'but be that as it may, I won't pay up until you get the roof fixed.'

The laird told the miller he had to pay up or leave the mill, but he refused to do either. His family had been in Lethnot for generations, and if the feckless drunken Lindsays hadn't driven them away yet, he'd be damned if he'd let them start now.

'This will be the worse for you, you mark my words!' cried the laird as he mounted his horse and stormed away, back to his big house at Edzell. There he brooded over what was to be done about Black, plotting a way to get this troublesome tenant out of his life once and for all.

As the laird lay awake, he heard a noise downstairs, a bumping around the back door, as if someone was trying to get in. When he went down and cautiously opened the door he saw Cobb, a local ne'er-do-well, skulking in the darkness. The laird knew that Cobb was probably trying to break in, to find some orna- ments he could sell to keep himself in drink, but the sight of the man had given him an idea.

'Come in, man!' called the laird. 'Just the lad I wanted to see. I have a job for you. Do you know Black, the miller? He's been a thorn in my side lately, and no doubt all his neighbours would say the same. You could say it would be a public service to see him gone for good … no matter how that were to occur. Do you think that's a job you'd be up to?'

'Well, how much would it be worth?' asked Cobb.

'Twenty pounds,' the laird said. And he explained his nefarious plan. He would go to back to the mill and tell Black that he had been hasty in his decision earlier. He would say he intended to see the repairs were done, but since Black himself would be best placed to make the arrangements, he should come up to Edzell that evening, and the laird would have the money for him there.

On Black's return to the mill, the laird explained, it would be dark, and he would have to walk along the side of the West Water where there was a steep drop down to the river below. If Cobb hid by the side of the road, he could ambush the miller, give him a dunt on the head, and take the twenty pounds from his pocket, then see to it that it looked as if poor Black stumbled and fallen into the river in the dark. This way, the laird thought, it could hardly be traced back to either of them.

And so this is what they did. The following evening, Black made his way up to the laird's house, where he was given twenty pounds with a cheerful smile. As he made his way back home in the dark, Black thought something was not quite right – what could have made the laird have such a change of heart? As he made his way along the side of the West Water, Cobb leapt out from the dark and was upon him. All the miller saw was a shadow lurching towards him. But he was quick, and threw his arms around the figure. The two men were locked in a deadly struggle. Cobb had the edge in sheer strength, but he also knew that if he hurled Black straight from the cliff, he'd be saying goodbye to his twenty pounds as well. But the miller's only thought was survival, and he kept trying to shove Cobb towards the drop. They wrestled and grappled without saying a word to one another, fighting until they were both tired. Then Black found a last drop of strength within himself, and with a final heave he sent Cobb down over the cliff into the roaring water.

Now, the laird was most confused – and sorely disappointed – when in a couple of days he saw the mill bustling with activity, as Black sorted out a new roof for the place. There had been no sign nor word from the assassin. Not unusual, perhaps, as he was a man of irregular habits. But a few days later, Cobb's body was found floating in a pool a little bit down the river. It was then that Black decided he should come forward and tell the story of what happened that night, and how he had had to force Cobb over the cliff in self-defence. No one doubted a word of his story – it was well known that Cobb had been a man involved in dark things. And as for the laird? Oh, Black suspected he had a part in it too, but he had no proof to bring forward. But the laird saw in Black's eyes that he suspected, and he never quite got rid of the fear that his role would come to light for the rest of his days. The story of the fight was a well-known one in Lethnot for many years after. The cliff where it took place was known ever after as Cobb's Heugh, and the pool in the rushing West Water below was known as Black's Pot.

The Shepherd's Wife of Glen Clova

A young shepherd named Donald MacAllister came over the hills from Glenshee, looking for work in Glen Clova. He got a place working for a farmer in the glen and settled into his new home. Donald was quiet and serious, and kept himself to himself. He never went to any of the dances at Halloweens or Hogmanays, though he was always invited. Donald's only social outings, if you could call them that, were his weekly visits to church each Sunday, and the occasional afternoon he spent discussing spiritual matters with the old minister, Ramsay. So Donald was not the most popular man – in fact, he was held in some suspicion by the folk of Glen Clova. But the man was dedicated to his work, that was certain. Whatever the weather, he would be out there making sure every sheep was accounted for. And this turned out to be a great stroke of fortune.

One winter's day, when Ramsay the minister had been attending the death-bed of an old cottar who lived over towards Glen Prosen, he was making his way back along the path which joins the glens, known as the minister's road, when snow started falling thick and fast. Ramsay lost the path in the white-out, and he wandered for hours trying to find his way again. Eventually, with the cold setting in about his bones, he had no choice but to huddle against a rock and pray that he would survive the blizzard. It was here that Donald came across him, now lying unconscious, as he searched for his sheep among the snowdrifts. The young shepherd took his plaid off, wrapped the minister in it, and carried him back to his hut, where a roaring fire and hot broth brought the old man back to life.

Although Donald was not one to boast of his own doings, it wasn't long before this tale of heroism had spread throughout the glen, and Donald MacAllister took on a new light in his neighbour's eyes. The young women of the glen were especially impressed, and none more so than Alice Grant, a servant lass on the farm next to Donald's. She became completely besotted with the quiet, heroic shepherd.

Alice was her mother's only child, and her father had been dead for many years. Most of the hours Alice was not working were spent caring for her old mother, who was not in good health. Despite her poverty, Alice's mother was a thrifty woman, and had saved most of the little money she'd ever had. Folk said that whenever Alice got the time to marry, the man would be sure of a good housewife and a good tocher to go with her.

Alice became the first to volunteer to go up to the hills and bring the shepherds their midday pieces, and she always made sure to visit Donald last, so they could spend some time talking and joking together. But she always doubted whether Donald thought of her any differently to any other girl, and she did her best to keep her feelings to herself until she was sure. One day, though, Donald remarked that she would certainly make a good wife to a man someday, and she couldn't help but sigh.

'Can you no see that the only man I've any care for is the one beside me now?'

Despite his quiet ways, Donald had been feeling the same, and straight away he asked Alice to be his wife. But he said the wedding could not take place for some time. He did not want to see Alice's old mother left alone if she became too busy with her own family, so he said that they could only marry after her mother's death.

As the weeks and months went on, Alice's thoughts began to trouble her. What if Donald was only interested in the money which would come to her when her mother died? Or what if her mother lived on for years more, and Donald found someone else in the meantime? There was no shortage of other girls who were interested in him, other lassies whose lives were not tied up in a constant whirl of work and care. Would she ever be free to make her own way in the world? Alice barely slept. It began to feel unbearable when she realised that one of her fellow farm servants was visiting Donald in the evenings while she was at home, answering her mother's constant calls for help. She had to do something.

Eventually, exhaustion and desperation drove Alice to a terrible answer. She went out to the hills one morning before work and gathered a bunch of deadly henbane, which she brewed into a potion, and each day she added a few drops to her mother's tea. It was not so much as to seem suspicious, but over the weeks her illness worsened, and before a month was out, Alice's mother was buried in Clova kirkyard.

Alice and Donald were soon married, and Donald had a good tocher of fifty guineas with his bride. But a few of the guests noticed Alice seemed a bit uneasy at the wedding. The couple settled down to their married life, but soon rumours were flying through the glen. Elsie the midwife, who knew herbs better than anyone, said she'd seen Alice with a suspicious looking bundle one morning, and wasn't the timing of old Mrs Grant's death convenient? It certainly was, everyone agreed. And although no one dared say a thing to the couple's faces, these things don't stay unheard for long in a small glen. One day, Donald was passing the byre on his way up to the hills when he overheard the milk-maids' conversation.

'Do you think Donald kens his wife poisoned her mither to get him?' one asked.

'Oh aye,' her friend replied, 'I bet he was as keen for the tocher as she wis to get free of the puir auld wife.'

It was the first he'd heard of this story, but Donald knew in his heart that something was troubling Alice. He'd thought she was still grieving, but perhaps it was guilt. When he got home that night, the look on his face told Alice that he'd heard what everyone was saying. She broke down and wailed her confession.

'It's true, it's true,' she sobbed, 'but it was all for love of you that I did it!'

'How could you do it, Alice?' he shouted. 'I canna love a murderess!'

Hearing these words, she ran for the door and out into the rainy night. She had no plan for where she was going, but soon she came to the River South Esk, roaring through the glen in full spate. Torn apart with guilt and grief, Alice threw herself into the freezing water. It was three days before she was found, miles downstream at a little pool above the Mill of Tray.

Donald could not stay in a home that held nothing but bad memories, so he took to the road again and left Glen Clova for good. But Alice, in the end, could not move on. Her ghost was seen wringing her hands by her mother's grave in the kirkyard at Clova, and the shepherds heard her wailing over the hills at night. Although old minister Ramsay prayed for her forgiveness so her spirit could rest, the ghost of Alice Grant has haunted the glen for many generations since.

The Shot of Bentyre

Many years ago, there was a small village called Bentyre near the head of Glen Doll. Bentyre was not much more than a few cottages huddled under the White Bent hills in the shelter of a wide and deep corrie, the Corrie Whitebents. In one of these cottages lived an old man named Robert Ferguson. He was a lonely figure. Robert was a shepherd, and he had herded sheep on the hills of Glen Doll since he was just a boy.

Everyone knew the story of Robert's life. One day, when he was a young man in his teens, he was out on the hills with his flock. He'd just had a fight with his sweetheart, Janet, so he was in a bad mood, and in no state for company. Then an old beggar woman came up to him.

'Do you have any food for a poor old woman?' she asked him.

'I'm no here to feed an auld witch!' he said in a fit of anger. 'If you don't go away and gie me peace I'll set my dog on you.'

And at that, the woman cast her ragged hood down and stared at him with icy eyes.

'Witch, is it? Maybe you're right. And you will pay for that insult for a long time. You will end up alone yourself one day, laddie, and then you'll ken what it is to be helpless.'

Her words went deep into Robert's heart, and they stayed there. He worried over it for a long time, but when he told his family they just laughed and said he must have been in a dwam. But after that day, it was as if he was always half somewhere else.

Robert married Janet after all, and they had two sons. When the boys got old enough, they wanted to see the world, and went to join a ship at Montrose. Not long after, Robert and Janet got word that it had gone down with all hands. It wasn't too long after the sad news that Janet took ill and was dead herself. Folk thought it was the grief for her sons that had done for her. So Robert lived his lonely life, quietly getting older, and as the years went by he became so old he wasn't able to spend his days on the hills any more. The folk of Bentyre thought he might have just sat in his cottage and starved to death if they hadn't started bringing food in to him, he seemed to have that little life left in him.

But life went on outside of Robert's sad home. In those days there were far more people living in Glen Doll and Glen Clova than there are now, and people were always visiting each other up and down the glen. The talk on everyone's lips was that young John Whyte, who lived in the cottage just beside Robert's, was to be married to a local lass called Maggie, and they were going to take on a small farm together. The day of the wedding fell in early December, and it seemed the whole of Glen Doll was packed into John's cottage to celebrate the occasion. All apart from Robert.

The minister quietly left as the party got going, since he planned to visit a sick parishioner on the way back to the manse at Clova. Then he saw Robert Ferguson standing in his doorway.

'Aye, minister,' he said. 'You'll hae been at the marriage?'

'Yes, and I was sorry not to see you there too. Do you not find it melancholy, keeping to yourself so much?'

'Och, thae places are no for the like o me. But it's been a lang time since we've seen you up this way. Aye, a lang time. And it'll be the last. I'll no see you again, minister,' Robert said.

And with that, he stepped back into his cottage and closed the door. The minister was troubled by these words, but he had his duties to attend to, so he saddled up his horse and headed away. By the time he returned to the manse it was the dead of night. He tried to think about tomorrow's sermon, but Robert's words were still echoing in his mind.

Crack.

A deep, rumbling sound, like thunder, but very close, came echoing through the winter's night. Roaring and grinding sounds filled the air. He'd never heard anything like it before, dull and stern. Judgement Day crossed his mind. Well, if it was, that was what he was in the job for. The minister saddled up his tired horse once more and went into the night to find out what was happening.

As he rode up the glen, the night was now dead quiet. It seemed nothing had changed since he passed by earlier. There was the old castle of Clova, the farm of West Bonhard ... But then he came up to Bentyre. Or he came to where Bentyre had been, just a few hours earlier. Now there was nothing but a heap of rocks and scree. The whole face of the cliff above Corrie Whitebents had given way, and come crashing down onto the cottages, taking everyone from young John and Maggie with their hopes and plans, to old Robert. The minister's blood ran cold as he remembered how Robert had spoken as if he saw it coming.

Strong men dug for a fortnight trying to find any survivors in among the wreckage, but after a while the people of the glen had to accept there could be none. The only living thing to escape the disaster was a cockerel, who perched atop the rocks and crowed at each empty dawn for weeks afterwards. After a month or so, the cockerel died too, and Bentyre has been silent ever since.

SLEEPING LADY LINDSAY

Lady Lindsay of Edzell was dead. She had a peaceful passing at home in Edzell Castle, and although it was unexpected, she was not exactly a young woman. So the family was, of course, sad, but not unduly disturbed. The greatest care was taken in laying Lady Lindsay out for her interment in the family vault. She was dressed in her best blue gown, her hair was combed, and her favourite jewelled rings were placed on her fingers.

The night before her funeral, the sexton went into the family chapel to make the final preparations for the burial, and to set Lady Lindsay in her coffin. As he went about his business, he could not help but feel sorry that the jewels she wore were about to be condemned to an eternity below ground. Their worth was just a trifle to the Lindsays, but it could make his and his family's lives secure. He knew he was the last person who was going to see her.

The sexton took Lady Lindsay's cold hand in his and gently pulled on a glittering ring. It would not slip off easily. He tugged harder, but no luck. But now the idea was in his head, the future brightening in front of him … and she was dead, after all. The sexton took his pocket knife and made a deep cut in Lady Lindsay's finger.

Ohhhh! The unearthly cry made his blood run cold. The sexton dropped his knife and stood aghast as fresh blood poured from her finger. *Alas, alas!* Lady Lindsay cried. And as the corpse began to sit up and untangle herself from her shroud, the sexton fell dead in a faint on the chapel floor.

Lady Lindsay took a moment to figure out where she was. Then she wrapped her bleeding finger with a rag torn from her own shroud, picked up a candle from the altar, and dragged the unconscious sexton out into the night, where the fresh air helped to revive him. Coming round and realising the situation he was in, he immediately fell to his knees again, begging her not to have him executed.

'But you saved my life!' she said. 'If you come up to the castle, I am sure my husband will see to it you get a good reward.'

But the sexton was too afraid, having heard of Lord Lindsay's unpredictable temper, and he dared not risk it. He begged to be allowed to leave in peace. Lady Lindsay said he must at least take the ring with her blessing, and, clutching the still bloody ring in his hand, the sexton made his way back to his family. His experience that night had unsettled him so deeply that he needed to put Edzell far behind him. Before the next day's sunset, the sexton and his family had boarded a ship at Montrose, making for a new life across the sea.

Lady Lindsay had a lucky escape, but this story would continue to haunt the family. Every few generations, there was a Lindsay who slipped into deep and impenetrable swoons – sleeps so deep that they could not be roused for days or weeks. She was not the only one of the family to be laid out for burial before their time. William Lindsay of Covington had a lucky escape when, moments before his funeral, his young great-granddaughter noticed his beard wagging. And it was not only the aristocratic branch of the family who were afflicted. Their poor cousin, Sleepin' Effie Lindsay of Cortachy, was known for her fortnight-long swoons. The last six weeks of her life were spent dead to the world, before finally she passed on permanently.

THREE CATERAN TALES

'Caterans' was the name given to bands of cattle-raiding warriors who used to come down from the Highlands and capture live-stock in the glens of Angus and Perthshire. The word comes from the Gaelic *ceatharn*, meaning 'fighter', and there was a time when hearing it would strike fear into the hearts of farmers and crofters. Here are three legends from the days of the Caterans.

The Battle of Saughs

The most notorious Cateran in Angus was a man who was known as the Hawkit Stirk. He had had this strange nickname all his life. As a baby, he had been abandoned at the door of the farmhouse of Muir Pearsie, at Kingoldrum. The wife of Muir Pearsie awoke one night to the sound of bleating cries. She elbowed her husband awake and whispered, 'Away doon and see whit that is!'

But he told her, 'Dinna be daft, it's naething but the croon o the hawkit stirk.' This was the orphaned calf that they were raising. Then he went back to sleep.

In the end, she got up herself and went downstairs, and there on the doorstep was a little boy wrapped up in a flannel cloth. They raised him as if he was their own child, and the nickname the Hawkit Stirk stayed with him all his days.

When he was a young man, the Hawkit Stirk left the farm and took to an outlaw life among the Cateran bands. He turned out to be a talented cattle thief, and he was soon the leader of his own band. It was about the year 1700 when he led this band in a raid in the parish of Fern. They rode in silently in the dead of a Saturday night, and they captured most of the horses and cattle belonging to the people there.

The next morning, folk awakened to find their fields and byres empty. Before the church service, the parishioners called a meeting in the kirkyard. People gathered among the graves and shouted about how desperate things would be if they couldn't get their cattle back. They suspected this was the work of the Hawkit Stirk, and thought it was about time someone taught him a lesson. But when the old minister asked if there were any volunteers to go after him, he got a dead silence.

But then young Macintosh of Ledenhendry leapt up upon a hillock and cried, 'Let those who will chase the Cateran follow me!'

Macintosh's friend James Winter was the first to come forward, but eventually most of the other young men in the parish joined them too. They gathered up all the weapons they could find, and the band set off north into the glens in chase of the raiders.

When they came to the banks of the Water of Saughs, they saw the Hawkit Stirk and his men. The Caterans had set up a camp around a roaring bonfire, and on it was roasting a fine young Fern cow. Macintosh strode up to the Hawkit Stirk.

'We'll no let our kye go without a fight. We ken the likes o you are cowards, stealing from folk while they sleep, but we'll have a fair fight for this lot. One on one.'

The Hawkit Stirk stood up and shook Macintosh's hand.

'A fair fight it is then.'

But his men were not listening. From somewhere in the huddle of Caterans, a shot rang out and hit one of the Fern men in the breast. He fell down dead, and all hell broke loose. The Fern men surged upon the Caterans and soon all were in the skirmish of battle. Macintosh and the Hawkit Stirk fought one another bitterly, and the young crofter was exhausted and losing strength. James Winter saw his friend was flagging, and he thought that the Caterans had forfeited their right to fair combat with that shot. Winter crept up behind the Hawkit Stirk and lopped his legs off at the knees with his broadsword. But even this was not enough to stop the Cateran leader. He fought bravely on upon his stumps, but he was weakened, and Macintosh thrust his sword through his heart.

Seeing the mutilation of their leader, the rest of the Cateran band fled in terror, though few managed to escape. Soon, the surviving Fern men were left with their cattle and a glen strewn with bloodied corpses. It was said that after that, Macintosh never went anywhere without his pistols, for fear the raiders would return to finish the battle and seek revenge for the Hawkit Stirk.

Macintosh of Ledenhendrie was rewarded for his bravery, though it did not bring him much peace. The Earl of Southesk made him Captain of the Parish of Fern. This did not go down so well with the previous Captain, a man named Ogilvie of Trusto. Trusto took a mortal hatred of Macintosh and vowed to see him off once and for all. He gathered a small band of men and lay in wait for Macintosh one night, by the side of the Paphrie Burn. But as Macintosh approached his ambush, his faithful dog stopped in his tracks and growled. Knowing something to be wrong, Macintosh quickly made for a hiding place in the crevice of a rock beside the river, where he hid under cover of darkness. Soon he heard his enemies approaching. They came by so close to where he was huddled that he could hear them whisper about their plans to kill him. Macintosh and the dog stayed crouched in the crevice the whole night, until they could safely make their way home in the morning. The cave where they hid has been known as Ledenhendrie's Chair ever since.

In Glenisla Kirkyard, the gravestone of Macintosh's friend James Winter stands as a commemoration of the Battle of Saughs, inscribed with the following lines:

Here lyes James Winter, who died in Peathaugh
Who fought most valiantly at ye Water of Saughs
Along with Ledenhendry, who did command ye day –
They vanquished the enemy, and made them run away.

Flora Cameron, the Rose of Glenesk

Flora Cameron lived in the parish of Lochlee, in a small cottage at Burnfoot, a mile or so from Tarfside in Glenesk, with her father James. She had been born far away from Glenesk, in Canada where her father had been a soldier and married a French woman. But Flora's mother had died giving birth to her, so once James left the army, he took his daughter back to the home of his childhood and they settled in the glens.

Although he was once again a poor cottar, James taught Flora to read and to play the fiddle. As she grew into a young woman, her beauty and talent led her to be known as the Rose of Glenesk. All the young men would have been glad to court her, but one in particular had fallen for her, young Ronald Maclean. Ronald lived at the house of Inchgrundle, at the north end of the loch which gives the parish its name. Flora took quite a liking to him herself, and it seemed certain the two of them would be wed.

Glenesk was often troubled by the Caterans in these days. They came in from Aberdeenshire, down the 'Devil's Staircase' by the Spittal of Glenmuick and into Glenesk by Lochlee. Sometimes they came by night and stole sheep and cattle under cover of darkness, but sometimes bigger bands came in with a trail of destruction, setting fire to crofts and byres as they steered the herds back north beyond the Dee. Black Donald More was the most feared of all the Caterans who came to Glenesk. He sometimes travelled in disguise, wearing a tattered plaid and taking the guise of a blind piper. He would go from house to house through the Angus glens, playing his pipes and accepting the hospitality of the crofters, while all the time he noted the layout of their crofts and his best route to plunder their livestock.

When Donald More came to Glenesk in this guise, his route took him to Burnfoot and to the house of James Cameron. He stood by the cottage and played some strains on his bagpipes.

Flora heard the music and came out, seeing what she thought was an old blind travelling musician from the Highlands. She listened, and spoke to Donald about the tunes he played, and gave him some of the little money she had before he went on his way.

Donald More, who was in truth neither blind nor old, added another house to his plundering route. The Camerons had no cattle he could steal, but he resolved to come back and capture young Flora Cameron and take her as his wife.

As he travelled onwards down the glen, he heard there was to be a tournament of games later that month in neighbouring Glen Clova, to mark the end of summer and the beginning of the harvest season. That would have the people of Glenesk distracted, especially the young men who might be able to fight his raiders off. It would be the perfect time to raid.

When the day of the games came, most of the folk of Glenesk took to the road to attend. Ronald Maclean was disappointed that Flora was not among them. Her old neighbour had fallen ill, and she had volunteered to stay at home and nurse her, to let her father get out and enjoy some of the celebrations. As the group climbed the mountain road which would lead them into the neighbouring glen, they had a good view of their homes below them. And to their horror they saw plumes of smoke rising up from the fields. They heard shrieks and sobs coming from those who had stayed behind.

James Cameron and Ronald Maclean led the charge back down the hill, both making straight for the cottage at Burnfoot. When they got there they saw Black Donald More himself, sweeping out of the cottage with Flora in his arms, tied up in a black cloak to stop her moving. Ronald drew his sword and yelled, 'Leave her, or die!'

Donald More cast Flora behind him and drew his own sword, lunging at Ronald. Two of his men came up from behind and grabbed James Cameron. As Ronald and Donald battled, Flora was doing her best to break free from her ties, and eventually she stumbled to her feet. Seeing this distracted Ronald for a second, and Donald More quickly knocked the sword from his hand. Then the Cateran raised his own sword and prepared to kill his rival. But as he thrust the sword towards Ronald's heart, Flora dashed between them, flinging herself into the battle to save her beloved. Donald's sword went straight through her, and she fell dead to the ground.

Ronald, now half mad with grief and fury, flung himself unarmed at the Cateran and hurled him to the ground. Donald's band of warriors were closing in, preparing to see off Ronald Maclean and save their master. But before they could reach him, Ronald sunk his teeth deep into the throat of Donald More, at the same time as Donald drove his sword into Ronald's belly. Before anyone could separate them, both men lay dead and bloody by the banks of the North Esk.

Craigendowie

The farmer of Craigendowie at Lethnot was well known to be a bit of a miser. He had a good stash of money somewhere, but nobody knew where he had hidden it. Even the Cateran raiders had heard about it, and on their next trip to Glen Lethnot they planned to raid his farm and steal his fortune. In the dead of night, they came and filled their sacks with all the meal and corn from his mill, loaded it onto Craigendowie's own horses, and sent them away northwards, with the best of his kye for good measure. A few of the robbers stayed behind to ransack the house in search of the gold.

They tried the house door, but it was well locked. So they broke open the shed and found a saw, which they used to saw down a tree in the yard, and then they used this as a battering ram and forced the door open. The Caterans opened every press and drawer in the house, and emptied everything onto the floor. There was no sign of anything valuable. They stoked up the fire and went up and grabbed the farmer out of his bed, and held his feet to the flames, demanding to know where his money was. Old Craigendowie would say not a word.

They could only think of one thing worse to do to him. The robbers grabbed his wife from the bed too, threw her over the back of their horse, and threatened to take her away along with the cattle. Still, the farmer said nothing.

Maybe he thought they weren't serious. So the Caterans decided to make clear how real their threat was by riding away with the old wife. They expected that any minute he would come running after them, to tell them where the money was in exchange for his wife's safety.

But by the time they had got three miles along the glen, they were so tired of the farmer's wife's endless complaining that they set her down and left her to walk back to her home. And the farm of Craigendowie was never troubled again by the raiders.

2

STRATHMORE AND THE SIDLAWS

The rich land of the Strathmore valley, once the heart of the Pictish kingdom, has drawn people to make their homes there for countless centuries. With the Mearns in the north marking a porous border with Aberdeenshire, the centre of Angus was once full of bustling farm toons (large farms which once employed enough men and women to make each farm its own community, with more than enough gossip to go round) and small textile towns like Kirriemuir, known as 'Thrums' after the weavers' threads. Although the land can now be worked with a fraction of the folk it once needed, Strathmore remains a farming place to this day.

FINELLA

Medieval Angus was ruled by the Mormaers, a line of earls descended from centuries of ancient Pictish kings. One Mormaer, Cruthneth, had a daughter named Finella. She was a strong-minded, ambitious and powerful woman. Finella set her sights on marrying the ruler of the neighbouring kingdom of the Mearns. They were wed and had a son named Cruthlint. He would grow up to rule both kingdoms and unite Angus and the Mearns as one land.

Finella had big plans for her son, but she was also fiercely protective. And it was a turbulent time they lived in, with plenty of chance for danger. Scotland had no hereditary king at that time.

When a king died, candidates from all the powerful families would battle with wit and sword to see if they could win the throne. King Kenneth II had won the throne after the death of his father, but there were plenty who saw themselves in it after him, and not all of them had the patience to wait for him to die of his own accord first. But he was determined to keep a steady rule over his kingdom.

Cruthlint grew up at his father's home at Fettercairn in the Mearns. He was young, and he knew that power was coming to him, and that gave him more confidence than his experience warranted. On a visit to his grandfather Cruthneth's home at Dalbog, on the banks of the North Esk, too much ale flowed and too many words were said. A fight broke out between Cruthlint and one of Cruthneth's young warriors. Cruthlint struck the winning blow, but it was a harsh one, and he killed the Mormaer's man.

The warriors of Angus were furious, and they wanted their revenge. The dead man's friends banded together and formed an army to come after Cruthlint and invade the Mearns. And Cruthlint wouldn't let it lie at that. He had men at his command too, and he led them to Dalbog to retaliate. And so the fighting went on. Instead of being united in prosperity, Angus and the Mearns were now more or less at war. Finella despaired of her son's lack of foresight, but she was glad to see that he could hold his own in battle.

King Kenneth soon came to hear of the fighting in the heart of his kingdom, and he vowed to put a stop to it. As if there weren't enough threats from outside without fighting one another! He summoned Cruthlint to appear before his court at Scone. The young man knew this wasn't a social invitation, and he decided his best bet was to avoid the king and lay low until he forgot his anger. He headed west towards the Highlands, where he thought he would not be found. But Kenneth had made up his mind to make an example of Cruthlint. He went after the

young man and soon caught up with him. And when he did, the
king slew Cruthlint where he stood.

When she learned of this, Finella flew into a fiery rage. How
dare Kenneth execute her son for a bit of youthful high jinks?
She swore that she would have her revenge. But unlike the men
in her family, she took her time thinking about how to do it.

After some time had passed, Finella invited Kenneth to her
husband's house at Fettercairn. She said that she too wanted
peace in Scotland, and she would like the two of them to come
to an agreement to make the future easier.

When Kenneth came to Finella's hall, he had to admit he was
impressed. She had had a statue made to honour her lost son,
and it was the grandest Kenneth had ever seen. In the centre of
the hall there stood a likeness of Cruthlint in shining bronze.
The statue had one hand outstretched, holding a glittering
golden apple, studded with red and green jewels. Kenneth gazed
at it in wonder.

'Go on,' said Finella. 'The apple is a gift for you, a peace offering. Take it, and then we will have some sport.'

Kenneth reached out and he laid his hand on the golden apple. It was the last thing he ever did. The pressure of his hand triggered the mechanism Finella had hidden within the statue. In an instant it set off a volley of crossbows hidden around the edges of the room, peppering the king's body with bolts. He fell down dead to the floor.

This was war. Finella was a wanted woman, and there was no tricking her way out of this one, but she did not regret it for a moment. Finella fled from the house and leapt onto her best horse, thundering off towards the coast. But the king still had loyal soldiers, and they were never far behind her. When Finella came to St Cyrus, she leapt down from her horse, thinking she might lose them in a wooded den. Her feet fell lightly among the tree roots, and she sped quickly through the forest. But the soldiers were fast too. She could hear their hounds howling after the scent of her. They were gaining on her, and ahead of her was a deep gorge where a waterfall thundered down over steep rocks. There was no way forward. They were going to catch her.

They were not, Finella decided. She picked up speed again and ran to the edge of the ravine. Then, as the soldiers watched with gaping mouths, she leapt. High up into the air she went and down into the depths of the falls, never to be seen again. To be dashed against the rocks was a far better death for a woman of the Pictish line than to die in defeat. The site of her leap is known as Den-Finella to this day.

JAMES THE ROSE

This tale was once well known by all around Auchterhouse, and it is still sung in ballad form too. At the beginning of the story our hero, Sir James the Rose, is fleeing from his enemies. James had defeated a fellow knight in battle, but this man had powerful friends, and now they sought revenge. The leader of James's hunters was a man named Sir John Graeme.

James's love, Matilda, lived at Auchterhouse Castle. He and his servant Donald made their way there in search of shelter. They arrived in the dead of night, and James tapped lightly on Matilda's bedroom window so he didn't wake the whole household. When Matilda appeared at her window, he whispered his story to her and asked if she would hide him.

'They'll know to look here for you,' Matilda told him. 'There's a place above the mill by Lundie Crags you can hide. Go there tonight, and I will come to you there at first light so we can escape together.'

Sure enough, as soon as James had sneaked away, there came a hammering at the front door of the castle. Matilda, already awake, was first to the door. There stood John Graeme and his men.

'Has James the Rose come by here?' he demanded. 'He has killed my friend and we will have justice.'

Matilda said that yes, he had been there, but that was days ago, and he'd be well on his way north by now. But as she watched the knights discuss their next move, her mind turned to her family's declining fortunes and the threadbare, draughty halls of the castle. And then she thought about the prospect of a life spent with James, always on the run from some enemy, no peace to be found. Her heart faltered. As they started to leave, she called after them.

'If you promise me a reward, I will help you!'

Sir John Graeme swung his horse round immediately. 'If we find him, his purse is yours.'

'Try the bank above the mill at Lundie Crags,' she said, and the riders thundered off into the night. Before long, they came upon the sleeping James and his servant Donald, wrapped in their plaids on the ground. One of the men drew his sword and would have beheaded James in his sleep, but John Graeme put out a hand to stop him.

'I won't have it said that I slew a sleeping man.'

So they formed a circle around James and waited for him and Donald to awake to that terrible sight. But they were not so honourable that they left James armed. While he slept, they took his sword and the knife from his belt. When James woke, he reached for his sword but found it gone.

'At least have the decency to give me a fair fight,' he said to John Graeme.

'You showed no mercy to my friend and we will show you none now,' he replied. James knew this was the end. He took his purse and handed it to Donald.

'You have been faithful to me,' he said. 'There's only one task left for you now, and that's to carry my body home. This will be some payment to you for that.'

Donald took the purse, and he watched with tears in his eyes as John Graeme's men slew his master. After that, John Graeme cut James's heart from his chest and carried it back to Auchterhouse Castle. He called Matilda to the door.

'We found him,' said John. 'We could not take his purse, but I have brought you his heart as a token.' And he handed the bloody lump to Matilda.

Matilda realised then what she had done. She clutched the heart to her breast, and she sobbed and sobbed. After that, she walked off into the hills towards the crags of Lundie, and she was never seen again.

In his Auchterhouse history Annals of An Angus Parish, *W. Mason Inglis notes another version of the story sometimes told. In this one, Matilda remains faithful to James, but Graeme finds him anyway, and she kills herself in grief after his death. Both the lovers were said to have died at a spot in the grounds of Auchterhouse Castle marked by a large willow tree. There are also other versions of the ballad which place the action elsewhere, but in Angus we know Auchterhouse is its true location.*

THE BOWMAN'S CONTEST

Finavon Castle is a ruin now, but it was once the seat of the Lindsays, one of the two powerful ruling families in Angus. The only family who could match them for wealth and power were the Ogilvies. The Lindsays and Ogilvies are known as bitter enemies, but this was not always the case. This is the story of how their friendship ended.

One midsummer, when the days were long and clear, Lindsay of Finavon held an archery contest at his castle. He decorated the lawn with flags and shining banners and set out a row of targets. In the grounds of Finavon Castle grew a huge chestnut tree, and around it he built a platform covered in gold cloth, where Lady Lindsay and her ladies-in-waiting would sit, waiting to present a crown of flowers to the winning archer.

Twenty-four noblemen came to compete for the prize that day. Among them was young Donald Ogilvy, and his father, Sir John Ogilvy of Inverquharity. The Lindsays and Ogilvies were all talented archers. Lindsay hit a perfect bullseye in the centre of one of the targets. Then young John fired his own arrow in such a way it knocked Lindsay's arrow to the ground and took its place in the centre. Cheers echoed around the lawn, but the main event of the contest was still to come.

Lindsay had a falconer with twenty-four falcons. One by one, the falconer would release the birds, and each archer would take his shot, aiming to strike down his falcon as it flew off. Lindsay himself took the first shot, and he hit the bird straight in its heart. He held the falcon up to the cheering crowd. As the others tried their hand, none had the same success. Most of the birds flew off alive. But the last to shoot was John Ogilvy. He fixed the falcon in his sight, and with the same deadly aim, shot his bird down dead. The crowd whooped and stomped. The contest seemed to be a dead draw between Lindsay and Ogilvy, but they would not leave without proving who was the better archer.

Before a final contest was held, the archers stopped to enjoy a grand feast. There was music and dancing and plenty of the finest wine. By the time the company reassembled, both the star archers were clearly the worse for drink. But neither was ready to give up his shot at victory.

During the feast, Lindsay devised a test that would challenge them both. He got the falconer to bring forth one more bird, and he called for one of his servants to come and stand on the lawn, as still as he could. The falconer placed the bird upon the servant's head.

Lindsay took up his bow and arrow and aimed. But his drunken fingers fumbled and he missed the bird, sending his arrow straight into the servant's eye. The crowd fell silent in horror. Before anyone could move, Sir John Ogilvy stepped up

and shot an arrow, and the falcon fell dead to the ground. As the servant began to scream in pain and others rushed forward to attend to him, Ogilvy stepped up to the platform to claim his crown from Lady Lindsay.

Lord Lindsay was devastated, not for his servant but for his pride. He returned to the wine to drown his sorrow, and the triumphant Ogilvy joined him to celebrate.

'I would not have missed if that man could have stayed still,' he muttered.

Hearing this, Ogilvy cried, 'Well, I will not have you think you had unfair play! I will challenge you again and trust me, I will win again!'

'I never turn down a challenge,' Lindsay replied.

Another servant and another falcon were brought into the hall. Lindsay took aim, and it was worse than before. His arrow pierced the poor servant's skull and he fell down dead. Ogilvy roared for another man to be brought in for his shot, and once more he hit the bird dead on.

Lindsay was furious.

'If I was not in my own hall it would be you I shot through the head!' he shouted.

'You couldn't hit my head if it was a mile wide,' said Ogilvy. 'But if you're not scared, we'll go out to the Lemno Burn at the back of the castle and see how we go.'

The two of them made their way to a spot on the riverbank known as the Kelpie's Haugh, each accompanied by a few supporters. It was now near midnight, but the midsummer night was lit by a full moon and they could see as well as they had at noon. They laid aside their bows and arrows, and each drew his sword. Lindsay was stronger, but Ogilvy was more agile, and still more sober. They cut and thrust at one another, shifting around the riverbank until Ogilvy was dazzled by the moonlight shining into his eyes. Then, with a flick of his wrist, Lindsay knocked his rival's sword from his hands and sent it flying away into the depths of the Lemno Burn. Ogilvy was defenceless. Lindsay roared in anger. He raised his sword above his head. The watchers braced themselves to see Ogilvy's head split.

But Lindsay let out one more furious shriek, then fell silent. He collapsed back onto the riverbank, stone dead. Ogilvy and his friends left Finavon immediately, and after that night, the two families never visited each other in friendship again.

THE LAIRD OF BALMACHIE

North of Carnoustie, there is a farm named Balmachie, which was once home to the Laird of Balmachie and his wife. One

morning, the two of them awoke at dawn as usual, and the laird
arose and began to prepare to head to Dundee to see to some
business. But his wife did not get up. She groaned and covered
her head with the blankets and said she was feeling terribly ill.
She told him that she would have to stay in bed that day, but
she was sure she'd be fine, and he should still go into Dundee
as he'd planned. So the laird told their servant to keep an eye on
her throughout the day, and off he went. He thought no more
about it until he was on his way back home in the evening, and
the sun was sinking in the sky.

As the laird rode north out of Dundee in the gathering gloaming, he passed Carlungie, where a Pictish souterrain lies among
the soft green hillocks. There, he stopped his horse dead in its
tracks. For in front of him there was a procession of tiny fairies
making their way across the path. Between them they carried a
litter, and on it he could see the shape of a human figure wrapped
up in blankets. The laird was terrified. But he remembered the
old stories his granny used to tell – she had always said that iron
was fatal to the fairy folk. He drew his sword and rode forward to
the fairies, and laid the blade across the litter.

'In God's name, let your captive go!' he cried.

At once, the fairies dropped the litter to the ground and
fled into the safety of the hills. The laird stepped down from
his horse, and he unwrapped the blankets around the figure
on the litter. He was stunned once more, for the face looking
back at him was none other than that of his own wife, pale and
unconscious. He wrapped her back up to keep her warm, and
balanced her in front of him on the horse to steer their way
home. He had a feeling things might not be quite finished with
the fairies, so he stopped at a neighbour's house and asked them
to keep an eye on his wife. Then he strode forward to Balmachie
to see what awaited him.

When the laird got into his house, he went straight upstairs
to the bedroom. He would have sworn the figure lying in the

bed was his own wife. She looked absolutely identical. But he knew she must be a fairy changeling. The laird asked the fairy-wife how she was feeling.

'Oh, I feel terrible,' she said. 'The bed is so cold, the servant hasn't been in to see me all day, I've been left all on my own.'

'That will never do,' he said. 'We must do something about that. Get up for a moment and I'll make up the bed again with warmer blankets.'

'I'm too weak to stand,' she whined.

'Then I will carry you,' said the laird. She protested, but he took her up in his arms, and made out that he was going to set her down in the armchair by the fire. But at the last minute he turned and thrust her with all his might into the flames. The fairy-wife let out an awful inhuman scream, but she did not burn. Instead, she bounced off the flames as though they were made of rubber. Then she went flying up with such force that she shot straight through the ceiling and away up into the sky, leaving a big gaping hole in the roof.

The laird waited for a little while to make sure she would not return. Then he went back to their neighbour's house, where he found that his real wife was now awake and very confused. The last thing she remembered, she told him, was a swarm of wee folk appearing at the bedroom window that morning. They had come in and surrounded her on the bed, but after that her memory was blank, until she had woken up here a few minutes earlier. She had awoken at the same moment the laird thrust the fairy impostor into the fire.

After that day, the wee folk never came back to bother Balmachie again. But no matter how well that hole in the ceiling was repaired, on each anniversary of the day the fairies came, a stormy wind would rise up and open the roof up again in the same place.

The Denfiend Clan

Travellers used to fear taking the road by Monikie, where a natural ravine near the burn was known as Denfiend – or the Fiend's Den. Everyone had heard of somebody who had taken this road and never returned. The place was known as the Fiend's Den because it was home to a dreaded family. There lived a clan of cannibals who lived on human flesh. The family became expert hunters. They would sneak out, overwhelm people from behind, and drag travellers back to their home, where they roasted them over a bonfire, devoured their flesh and tossed their bones in a heap in the corner. Although the Denfiend clan were not particularly fussy – they'd eat anyone – they did prefer their meat young and tender. Children were their favourite delicacy.

Although for a long time nobody knew what was getting hold of all the travellers who passed Monikie, it was clear that something was very wrong there, so of course people stopped taking that road. Cut off from their ready supply of fresh meat, the clan grew hungry. They took to raiding the nearby village and farms. The cannibals crept in and lay in wait to snatch children on their way back from the fields.

But they got a little too confident about coming close to the village. One day, the father of the cannibal family was spotted racing away with a child under his arm, and the militia were called up from Dundee to track the Denfiend clan to their lair. There they found the father, his wife, and an array of their family – there were old grandparents, grown sons and daughters, and even a wee lass who was just one year old.

The family was taken into the city to stand trial, but the bones littering their floor were evidence enough. All of the Denfiend clan were sentenced to execution but one. The judge thought the little girl was young enough to be reintroduced into society. If she could reach adulthood without following in her family's footsteps, she would go free.

The magistrates found a foster family in Dundee who agreed to raise her. But as she got older, they noticed she only ate things like soup and tatties with reluctance. She preferred to eat meat, but even mutton or beef didn't seem to quite satisfy her. And when she was around other children, they had to keep a close eye on her. She was definitely a biter …

So one day, when the girl was coming to the end of her teenage years and a local child went missing, everyone knew where to look. The last of the Denfiend clan was sentenced to be burnt in the Seagate for the same crime that had seen her family die eighteen years before. Crowds of people gathered round, booing and hissing for the horror of her crimes. But she remained perfectly calm and composed. Turning to face the crowd, she spoke.

'Why do ye chide me as if I had committed a crime? Give me credit, if you had the experience of eating human flesh, you too would think it so delicious that you would never forbear it again.'

And so she died, with no sign of repentance.

There are several versions of this story, some of which place the cannibals' home elsewhere in Angus at the Glack of Newtyle, or at Auchtertyre. The girl's refusal to repent is shared between them all.

ॐ

CARNEGIE'S SHADOW

In the seventeenth century the Earl of Southesk was named James Carnegie. Carnegie lived at Kinnaird, by the South Esk river which gave the family their title. He was famous as a skilled fighter, and he was no ordinary swordsman. In those days, all young Scotsmen of good breeding were sent to continental Europe to complete their education, though young James Carnegie had had a better education than most. He learnt his skills in Padua at a school of the black arts, and he had none other than the Devil himself as an instructor.

The Devil gives nothing away for free, especially knowledge. The fee he claimed for teaching was one soul a year. When the school term finished for the summer, the Devil bade the class all line up along the classroom wall. He told them that when he clapped his hands they were all to run for the door. The unlucky boy who was last to reach it would be that year's sacrifice.

One year, it was young James Carnegie who stumbled and reached the door a few seconds after his classmates. Looking behind him, he saw the hungry face of his teacher looming.

'I'm no the last!' he cried. 'My shadow is ahint me!'

This was true enough. The Devil snatched for his shadow and ripped it clean off, but James made it home to Kinnaird that summer.

From that day on, Carnegie never had a shadow, though he tried to hide it by keeping his house in darkness and walking in the shade. And the Devil never forgot that he had been tricked. When James Carnegie grew old and finally died, his former teacher returned to claim what he'd been owed all these years. Before Carnegie could be given a Christian burial, the Devil swept up to Kinnaird in a black coach led by six black horses and snatched his body up. He bundled Carnegie into his coach and thundered out to the Starney-Bucket Well, by the family's burial ground. The Devil's coach drove right down into the depths of the well and back down to Hell. It seems the Starney-Bucket Well still leads down to the underworld, for on some dark stormy nights, James Carnegie can be seen emerging from it in the Devil's coach. He circles around Kinnaird, keeping a wary eye on his old family home, and then disappears back the way he came into the fires of Hell.

The Hermit of Kinpurnie

There was once a wild youth from Dundee named Davie Gray. Davie never darkened a kirk door, but he was a common sight around the estates at Camperdown, Balunie and Auchterhouse, poaching some fish or game. He could run like the wind, and his mind was as fast as his feet, so he always escaped the clutches of the lairds' gamekeepers.

Every laird in the Sidlaws hated his guts. They would have been happy to see him hanged, but they'd have to catch him first. One night they all got together at a dinner, where gossip and wine both flowed freely. As always, the talk turned to Davie Gray and how they could be rid of him.

The Laird of Kinpurnie, by Newtyle, suggested an unusual idea. He was building a tower at the top of Kinpurnie Hill, to decorate his estate. It was fashionable then for such towers to have a hermit living in them, as a rustic and romantic living ornament. He thought that if he advertised for a hermit, with a handsome reward at the end of their stay, it was likely that Davie Gray would apply. But they could turn it into a true imprisonment, and make sure that he never left.

The lairds all agreed this was worth a shot, and they all gave money to finish building the tower. Soon, the Dundee bellman was walking through the streets of the town crying the news. A hermit was wanted for the new tower at Kinpurnie, and if he could stay seven years there, he would be paid one hundred pounds for each year.

Perhaps Davie thought this was his chance to get one up on the lairds again, or perhaps the idea of the fortune was just too tempting. He went to Kinpurnie to apply, and he was told he could start that very day. The Laird of Kinpurnie took him up to the tower and handed Davie a sheepskin which was to be his only clothing for the next seven years. There was a rough bed on the floor, and he would get a small meal of bread and water each day. But he would have no fireplace, no water to wash and nothing to comb or cut his hair. Even his nails could not be cut. And the few people that Davie would see, he was absolutely forbidden to speak to.

The lairds hoped that a few months of this life would be enough to break his spirit, or even kill him off for good. But Davie Gray took to the life of a hermit well. Though he had no fire, he paced up and down his cell to stay warm through the winter, and though he did not speak he sang to keep his voice from fading, learning the tunes the birds sang in the trees. Even with only cold bread and cold water to sustain him, he refused to be downhearted.

Soon Davie's fame spread, and people began to come from around Scotland to see the famous Hermit of Kinpurnie. He was more isolated, more deprived by far than any other hermit in the land. Year after year, Davie kept on pacing his cell and singing to himself. When the end of his sixth year came, the Magistrates of Dundee took a trip up to see for themselves, not quite believing that he still lived. He sang out to them through the tower window that he would see them all again next year.

And in another year's time, to the amazement and fury of the lairds, Davie was still there. They came to see him released, and so did a huge crowd of folk from all around who were keen to see what seven years alone had done to Davie. The crowd whooped and cheered for him as the door was unlocked. Davie staggered out into the sunlight. His hair and beard straggled down to his knees. Instead of the jet black they had been when he went in, they were now snow white. The nails on his fingers and toes had grown long and yellow and curved like the claws of a seagull. Among the crowd were many friends of his from the years before, but as Davie looked around, dazzled in the sunlight, he didn't recognise a single face.

When he tried to speak about his experience, his words sounded strange and stilted from lack of use. But his voice flowed strong and clear when he made the sounds of the hill. Davie could caw like a crow or low like a cow, sing like a thrush or bark like a fox, and he could even perfectly echo the sighing sound of the wind in Kinpurnie's trees. These were his words now. He was somehow less and more than human, a part of the hill itself.

But Davie was a hero to the people of Dundee. He had survived and he had won the lairds' money. A coach took him through the streets of the city, where he was cheered and welcomed. They found a comfortable house for him to stay in, and doctors came to help him bathe and cut his nails, and told him what to eat to bring his strength back. They thought he would begin to thrive after some time back in the normal way of life.

But a week or two after his release, Davie seemed to be getting weaker instead of stronger. He had no appetite for food, and no energy to walk. Language did not come back to him. Instead, he avoided the company of people wherever he could, and when he was spoken to his only answer was to make the sounds of the hills, over and over. Within a year of his release, Davie Gray contracted a fever, and was gone from the world of men forever.

THE FUNERAL

This is a Traveller story which Sheila Stewart told, and included in her book *Pilgrims of the Mist*. She heard it while staying not far from Forfar.

A Traveller family were camped on the road between Forfar and Montrose, when the husband awoke one day to find his wife was dead. She was only about forty, so her death came as a surprise to the family. Her daughter, who was about twenty, was absolutely devastated by the news. As she wept over her mother's body, she sobbed, 'I wish that God had taken me instead!'

Nothing her father could say made any difference. He hoped that she would start to feel better after a good cry, but the girl could not be consoled. She kept sobbing over and over that she wished she had been the one to die. And although he was grieving too, it worried her father to hear her talk like that.

He told her that her mother would have wanted for her to go on living her life. Death was one of those things that comes into every life sooner or later, he said, and no one has the power to change it. We just have to try and keep going on. His daughter wiped her eyes on her sleeve, and she said that she supposed he was right. But the shock of her mother's death coming so suddenly was hard for her to take.

The law said that Travellers had to go and report any deaths at the nearest police station, so the man made his way into Forfar, while the girl stayed in the tent thinking over her memories of her mother. Soon, the police sent up a horse and cart to take the body down to the mortuary. When they went to take her away, the man asked the police officer not to close down the lid on her coffin for a while, to give all her relatives a chance to come in and say goodbye before the funeral.

The police officer was not keen to do any favours to a Traveller, and he wanted to get the burial out of the way as soon as possible. But the man put his foot down. He sent word around to all his wife's family, and his own family, that the funeral would be held soon. They didn't have much money, and she was to be buried in a pauper's grave, but they were determined to give her a proper goodbye.

The day before the funeral was set to take place, the dead woman's family all gathered outside the police mortuary in Forfar, taking turns to go in and pay their respects. Her daughter had asked to be the last one to go in and see her mother, just before they put the lid down on the coffin.

When she was in the little room with her mother, the young woman stayed for a long time. She held her mother's hand and spoke to her in a low voice. And when she stood up to leave, she bent down and laid one last kiss on her mother's forehead. But when she lifted her head up from the coffin, it was the mother who was standing there. The daughter was lying in the coffin instead.

The mother put her shawl over her head and walked out of the little room. There was a policeman waiting at the door, and as she passed by him, she told him it was time to put the lid on the coffin now. When she came out of the mortuary, all the family outside looked below her shawl. Their faces went white when saw the dead woman they'd said goodbye to moments before, walking around as if nothing was wrong.

The father ran back into the mortuary and started banging on the door of the room the coffin was in.

'Open up!' he shouted. 'You have to open the coffin!'

'Oh, for goodness' sake,' sighed the policeman. 'I've just this minute finished closing it.'

'You have to open it! I swear, this is important!' he insisted. By now the rest of the family had crowded into the room as well, and they all watched as the policeman prised the lid back off of the coffin. Lying inside it was the young daughter, as though it had been her who was dead all along.

Although nobody could ever figure out how this had come about, the daughter was dead, and the mother had many more years of her life to live.

THE GHOST OF FERNIEDEN

There's the Broonie o Ba'quharn
And the ghaist o Brandieden,
But o a' the places in the parish
The deil burns up the Vayne.

The Laird of Fern lived at Vayne Castle. He was a cruel man, and anyone who offended him faced a horrible punishment. Once, when he grew angry with a servant that he thought was lazy – though the man was nothing of the sort – he had him thrown into a dungeon and left him there until he wasted away in the dark. His body was buried secretly in the grounds of the castle, with no proper grave.

Until he buried the servant, the laird had known no guilt or consequences for his actions. But from that day on, he was a haunted man. All day and night the doors slammed in his house and the windows clattered in freezing winds that only he could feel. Worst of all, his ears rang with every scream and sob of sorrow and despair from all the victims that he had ignored in the past. He could do nothing but lie on his bed in torment and repent for his ways. The laird lived the rest of his life, which was not long, as a broken and exhausted man.

After the laird's death, his servant's spirit was still not fully at rest, but he wasn't a tormented ghost any longer. He could roam the parish freely, and he was happier than he had been for most of his life. He became known as the Ghost of Fernieden. As in life, he was a hard worker, and he liked to go around and help out on the farms in the parish. By night, he flitted around and left byres clean, neeps pulled up and stacked in neat piles, and straw ready thrashed. The farm servants were always amazed to come in in the morning and see the ghost's work.

But ghosts are a much misunderstood kind of people. Despite all his helpfulness, people still feared the Ghost of Fernieden. They had all heard rumours that he was a terrible sight, with teeth and claws dripping with blood, and people avoided going out at night in case they caught a glimpse of him.

One night, the ghost was on his way to work when he heard a big commotion inside a farmhouse. He listened at the door and heard the cries of a woman in great pain with a difficult birth. Why had nobody gone to fetch the wise old woman across the burn, who was the midwife and doctor to the parish? Then he heard one of the men say, 'If it was day we could fetch the midwife, but what if we met the ghost? We'd be done for ourselves and then there'd be nobody to help!'

So the Ghost of Fernieden took matters into his own hands. He slipped round to the stables and saddled up the grey mare that he knew was the speediest. He flew through the night until he arrived at the wise woman's door, and he chapped on the door, crying, 'Come quick! The farmer's wife at Fernieden is having a bad time wi her bairn!'

The midwife appeared in an instant, and he helped her up on the horse and off they went again, quick and quiet through the night. As they approached Fernieden, the woman tensed up behind him on the horse.

'I'm a bit feart,' she admitted. 'They say this is where the ghost haunts, and what if we were to come across him the night!'

'Ach, dinna be daft!' he replied. 'You'll no see any worse the nicht than what's in front of you right now.'

When they arrived at the door of the farmhouse, the ghost set her down, and promised he would return in an hour to take her home again. As they stood by the door, the woman looked at him properly for the first time. She noticed his very strange appearance.

'I never asked your name. Who should I say brought me here tonight, and how come you look so tired and sair?'

'Oh, I've wandered many a lang road in my day without horse or mare. And if they ask wha brought you here tonight, just say you rode ahint the Ghost of Fernieden himself.'

Thanks to the ghost, both the farmer's wife and her new son had a long and healthy life ahead of them. The ghost continued his night-works around the farms for years more, but he had been a ghost a long time, and it was tiring work. After a while he did not have the strength to work any longer, so he wandered the braes and thought about his short life and long death. He had been lonely for most of that time, and he stayed lonely, because most of the people of Fern were still afraid of him.

But when the little boy who had been born that night grew up, he didn't listen to the stories about the ghost. He wasn't afraid of going out at night, and he would walk over the braes in the dark to go to dances or visit friends. One such night he spotted the Ghost of Fernieden, wandering the paths by himself. And instead of running away, he walked over to the ghost.

'Good night,' he said, 'what is it brings you to be wandering out here?'

And finally, the ghost had someone to talk to. He told the boy the story of his life and the way he had died, and the boy listened with a sympathetic ear. And from that night on, no one saw the Ghost of Fernieden again. He could rest at last.

The 'Ghaist o Fernieden' was one of Angus's best-known ghost stories in the nineteenth century, and it is also popular in the form of a song or recitation. The helpful ghost takes on a role here which is often given to a Broonie in other folk tales. There is another, similar, story set at Farnell. In this one, the ford across the river between Farnell and Brechin was said to be haunted by the vengeful and bloodthirsty ghost of a traveller who had been killed there, and the community is afraid to go near the river at night. But a young girl ignores these warnings to fetch the midwife from Brechin for her sister, who is having a difficult birth one stormy winter's night. She has no horse but is offered a lift across the dangerous river to the midwife's house by a stranger on a strong horse – and of course, when she admits her fear of meeting the ghost to her helper, he replies, 'There's no fear of that, for I myself am the ghost of Farnell.'

One more story in this vein does have a Broonie as the hero, the Broonie of Claypotts, who you will meet elsewhere later in the book. In the days when Claypotts Castle was the home of the Claverhouse family, the Broonie once forded the roaring Dighty Burn by himself to fetch the midwife for the lady of the house when no one else could.

The Drummer of Cortachy

James Ogilvie of Airlie and Archibald Campbell of Argyll were powerful enemies. The two had been at odds with one another for years. When Argyll took up the cause of the National Covenant, and Airlie swore loyalty to King Charles I and his Church, the feud between them turned deadlier. In the summer of 1640, Airlie was called to go and fight with King Charles. He thought Argyll would be honourable enough not to attack his home while his wife was there alone. But he was wary of leaving her with no protection. Airlie employed a drummer boy, whose duty was to keep watch from the castle tower and beat a tattoo on his drum if he saw enemies approaching.

In the end, Airlie's suspicions proved true. Argyll wanted a victory more than he wanted an honourable one, and he led a charge on Airlie with a band of men and burning torches when he knew the man of the house was away. And no drumbeat came to warn Lady Airlie. The first she knew of the attack was when she heard the thumps of Argyll's men battering down her door.

Perhaps the young drummer boy had been exhausted from his long watch and drifted off at his post. Or perhaps Argyll had led a quiet approach, from an unexpected direction. But Lady Airlie was certain that he had stayed silent on purpose. She knew that his family were Camerons, and their public sympathy lay with Argyll's side in the war.

Lady Airlie sent her children hurrying out of the castle to escape, but she herself ran to the foot of the tower where the drummer boy was stationed.

'You think you can betray my family? I will show you where that will get you!' she roared up to him. And she fastened the huge iron bolts on the tower door, bolts that could only be opened from the outside. Then she ran out of the castle herself, to face her reckoning with Argyll.

As the flames consumed the tower of Airlie, the drummer boy beat a constant *rat-a-tat-tat* on his drum, and he cried his last words down to Lady Airlie.

'I swear, Ogilvy, that I will never fail to warn your family again. Never!'

After the ruin of Airlie, the Ogilvy family set up home at Cortachy Castle, a few miles north of Kirriemuir. Time passed, and the wealthy families of Scotland eventually forgot their trespasses against each other and settled back into high society. But the drummer boy did not forget the Ogilvies. From that day on, every death in the Ogilvy family was heralded by the eerie *rat-a-tat-tat* of a phantom drum.

Two centuries later, the seventh Earl of Airlie was in residence at Cortachy. He was married to Margaret Bruce, and Margaret was pregnant. The couple invited a cousin of hers, whose name was also Margaret, to stay at Cortachy for a night. The visiting Margaret came with her maid, Ann.

On the evening they arrived at Cortachy, Margaret was dressing for dinner in her room when she heard the sound of drums and fifes. It sounded very close, almost as if the musicians were inside the house, on the floor below her. Over dinner, she remarked to her hosts: 'What fantastic musicians

you have here! It is delightful to hear the drums as you go about the house.'

As soon as the words were out of her mouth, the earl went white. He dropped his fork, stood up, and left the table without a word of explanation. Dinner continued awkwardly. Margaret had no idea what was wrong, until a friend of the family quietly took her aside and explained the earl's odd reaction.

While the Earl and Lady Airlie and their guest had a more subdued breakfast the following morning, Ann was alone in the bedchamber, folding clothes as they prepared to leave. She was startled by the sound of footsteps. Then she heard the *rat-a-tat-tat, rat-a-tat-tat* of someone beating a drum. Ann peered out of the window in case the drummer was outside, but there was no one to be seen. Very strange, she thought, but she assumed the old castle carried sound in strange ways.

When Margaret said goodbye to her relative that morning, it was to be the last time they saw one another. Not long after returning home, she received a letter with the news her cousin had not survived the birth of her twins. Lady Airlie had left a note in her desk, written on the night of their visit. 'Margaret has heard the drummer, and I believe it is for me he drums.'

When Ann came in to find her mistress weeping, and heard the story of the drummer, the maid was astounded. 'But – I heard it too!' she cried.

The drummer of Cortachy has been heard many a time since then, and he follows the Airlie family wherever they go. In 1900, the ninth Earl of Airlie was in Bloemfontein, fighting in the Boer War. One of the officers was horrified to hear the military band playing one Sabbath morning. Had they no respect? When he upbraided them for this behaviour on Monday morning, he was met with bemused faces. Not one of them had touched their instruments all the previous day. But back at Cortachy, Lady Airlie had heard the music too. That Monday, the earl led an attack on the Boers, and was shot straight through the heart by his enemy.

THE NORTHMUIR CAIRN

The Northmuir lies around a mile north of the town of Kirriemuir. Being on the edge of the town's lands, this was where the irregular burials would be in days gone by, for people who could not be buried in the kirkyard. This was where the hanged criminals and suicides found their final resting place, marked only by a solitary cairn. That was reason enough for most people to give it a wide berth, especially at night.

Those who did dare to go near it usually only did so once, for the Northmuir was haunted by a terrifying and pitiful ghost. A tall, pale woman paced around and around the cairn all night long, sighing and sobbing. And worse, she held to her blood-stained breast a tiny, ghostly child. All night they would wander, until the first light of dawn came over the horizon, when she would flee from the sun and fade away.

The story of how the poor woman, and the cairn itself, came to be there is one from the days when wolves still roamed Angus. By Abernethen Well, there was once a castle, home to the Laird of Abernethen and his beautiful daughter. Each year, the laird held a wolf-hunt, and all the landed gentry of the area would join him. If they were successful – which they usually were – Abernethen would celebrate with a grand ball. It was at one of these balls that young Lord Lindsay of Finavon met Abernethen's daughter, and Lindsay immediately set about wooing her. The young woman soon fell for his charms, but Lindsay was not a loyal man. When she became pregnant to him, he abandoned her and set his sights elsewhere.

The girl was devastated, and her family had no sympathy for her. Her father banished her from the house, saying she brought nothing but shame to them. With no friends and nowhere to go, she wandered towards Kirrie. An old woman came across her shivering in the night and brought her into her cottage. She looked after the girl of Abernethen and gave her a safe, warm place to have her baby. But it was as if she was in another world. Her eyes looked through the old woman as if she hardly saw her. She was so broken with shame and sorrow.

One morning, the old woman awoke to find that the girl and her baby were gone. When she went out to look for them, her worst fears were confirmed. She found their bodies lying together. In her desperation, the girl had suffocated the baby, then cut her own throat. The two of them were buried in one grave at the Northmuir, with no stone or cross. But the people of Kirrie knew the tragedy was too great to go unmarked, so they carried stones to the burial place and raised the Northmuir Cairn in their memory.

JOCKIE BAREFIT

The laird of the lands around Finavon was a cruel and a ruthless man. His name was Earl Crawford, but he was known as Earl Beardie on account of his pointed, devilish beard – or as the Tiger Earl, for his temper. There were only two things in the world that brought Earl Beardie any joy. One of these was the beautiful Spanish chestnut tree which grew in the grounds of Finavon Castle. This was his pride and joy, an ancient tree grown from an acorn dropped centuries before by a Roman soldier. Sometimes the earl would walk around the tree and stand admiring it, one hand on its trunk. The only other thing that ever brought a smile to his lips was gambling. The earl would happily stay up all night drinking and playing cards, making wilder and wilder bets.

Living around Finavon at that time was a boy who made his living by taking messages between farms in exchange for a bite to eat or a barn to sleep in. The poor lad was an orphan, so no one knew his family name. He never had enough money to put together for a pair of shoes, so he was known as Jockie Barefit.

One day, Jockie had just left a farm and was on the lookout for his next job, when he saw a stranger ride up on a beautiful big black horse. The stranger stopped and looked down at Jockie.

'Are you the messenger boy around these parts?'

'Aye sir, that's me.'

The stranger reached into his pocket and pulled out a white envelope. This was something quite different to the scraps of paper Jockie was normally given. It even had a red wax seal.

'I need you to take this to Earl Beardie at Finavon Castle, and make sure that it is delivered.' He handed Jockie a big gold coin. It was more money than he'd ever dreamed of, never mind held.

'I will, sir, immediately!' Jockie bowed to the stranger and set off for the castle. When he got there, he rang the bell at the gates, and waited. There was no answer. But the man had been very insistent that it was delivered properly. So Jockie decided to loup the wall of the castle. He scrambled up the wall and lost his grip, falling down the other side and twisting his ankle. He stood up and found the pain was so bad he could hardly put weight on it – he needed a stick to walk with. Looking around for something he could use, he saw the chestnut tree, its branches spreading almost to the ground. Jockie limped over to the tree and broke off part of a branch to stick under his oxter. Then he made his way to the servants' door of the castle and knocked.

Earl Beardie's butler answered the door. He took the letter from Jockie and was about to shut the door in his face. But the earl was pacing his corridors and caught sight of the boy in the doorway. He stormed down to the door and shoved the butler out of the way.

'You, boy! Where did you get that stick?'

Jockie explained in a shaky voice that he had hurt his leg coming over the wall to see the letter got in safely, and that he'd needed a branch from the tree to help him walk. The look on

the earl's face was awful. Jockie would have run for his life if he could have. The earl grabbed his arm.

'So, you trespass on my land, and you damage my property! Go and fetch a rope,' he said to the butler. 'There's going to be a hanging.'

When they heard of this, the other servants begged the earl to show mercy for once. They knew Jockie and knew he was harmless. But he heard none of it. Earl Beardie saw that Jockie Barefit was hanged from the branches of that same chestnut tree. And because he had no family to bury him, they took his body out to the hill nearby and burnt it.

It was only after that, feeling pleased to see justice done, that Earl Beardie opened the letter Jockie had delivered. It was an invitation to a grand dinner at Glamis Castle the following week. The earl was delighted – he loved a chance to show off to the other nobility, and of course a drink and a game of cards were likely too.

When the night came round, the earl noticed a beautiful, big black horse among the others in the stables as he arrived – the best horse he'd ever seen. He guessed that it belonged to the only man he didn't recognise, a stranger whose dark features somehow matched the creature. As the night wore on and the guests staggered off to bed, Earl Beardie and this man were among the last ones standing.

'Are you a gambling man?' the stranger asked him.

'Aye, I am that,' said Earl Beardie. So they took a bottle of whisky and went upstairs to a quiet room for a game. As they dealt the cards, Beardie asked the man if that lovely black horse was indeed his.

'It's my horse,' said the man. 'But I tell you what, it's yours if you win tonight.'

'And what would you want from me?' asked the earl.

'I like to keep things interesting. If you lose, I'll tell you the forfeit then.'

A sober or a sensible man would have stopped there, but Earl Beardie was neither of these. They shook hands and set to playing. The earl had the worst night's luck of his life. He lost hand after hand, and it was soon plain to him he had lost the game. As he looked to the stranger to ask what his forfeit was, he noticed the hooves under the table, the horns at his temples. The earl was looking into the eyes of the Devil himself.

To this day, Earl Beardie is cursed to sit in that room, playing endless rounds of cards, and always losing. The room is long lost, but if you count the windows on the outside of Glamis Castle, you will always find one more than if you count them from the inside.

And as for poor Jockie Barefit – the ploughmen around Finavon used to say that, if they were out walking in the evenings, sometimes a young lad would fall into step with them on the road, a quiet lad who wore no shoes. And if he was with you when you came to the Lemno Burn, he would burst into flames and disappear.

Earl Beardie will never dee
Nor pair Jock Barefit be set free
As lang's there grows a chestnut tree.

3

Glamis Castle

Glamis Castle is the largest and, by a long way, the most famous castle in Angus. It has been home to the Lyon family, earls of Strathmore, for centuries. Over the years the castle, its family, and its rumoured secret room (which also features in the Finavon story Jockie Barefit) have picked up so many legends that they have earned their own section here. Today, Glamis Castle is best known for the shared dubious honours of being the most haunted building in all of Scotland, and for having been the childhood home of the Queen Mother.

The Walnut Tree

When the Lyon family first lived at Glamis Castle, the garden was famed far and wide. It was laid out with long tree-lined gravel paths, rich flower beds, beautiful water fountains, and fine marble statues. In the middle of the garden there stood a walnut tree with spreading branches, under which the fine folk of the house would sit in summer, listening to birdsong.

The head gardener retired, and it was hard to find someone who could replace him. A garden so beautiful demanded a special talent to take care of it. Lord Lyon asked around all of Angus, then all of Scotland, and he had a line of hopeful candidates at his door. But he didn't quite trust any of them to keep up his famous garden. Lyon heard that there was a renowned gardener in Holland, the favourite of the kings and queens of Europe. He sent a letter offering him a huge sum to come to Scotland and work at Glamis. So the gardener agreed and came to see the place, and he was impressed by Glamis too. He agreed to work there at once, and he made the garden even more beautiful than before. In his letters back home, the gardener said that Glamis's was a finer garden than any to be seen in Holland.

Now, this hurt the pride of some folk, particularly a rich young merchant in Amsterdam who rather fancied his own garden as the best not just in the country, but in the whole of Europe. The next time his business took him to the port of Leith, he headed north to see Glamis for himself. The merchant had brought his own principal gardener with him, and a few more servants besides, for he intended to make an impression. He wore his finest clothes, with gold embroidery glinting in the sun, and his whole party rode on horseback.

When they arrived at Glamis, Lord Lyon himself was not at home, but his daughter Lady Laura was, and she welcomed the strangers to the castle. Laura took them to see the famous garden, and she was soon as impressed with the merchant as he was with the landscape. They sat below the walnut tree and talked. The merchant's Scots was good after years of trading with Leith, and he had many stories from his travels. Lady Laura brought out cakes and wine, and they talked long into the evening. It was a midsummer night, when the twilight lasts all night, and that suited both of them just fine as they strolled and talked for hours.

Late that evening, another visitor came to the gate of Glamis. Donald Cameron of Lochiel had come down with a mind to court Lady Laura, and when he found her alone in the garden with a rich and handsome stranger – a foreigner, no less! – he was enraged. Cameron dragged Laura from her chair and the merchant, who thought the castle was under attack, rose up to defend her.

Cameron drew his sword. The merchant drew his own in defence. Soon they were fighting, cursing each other in Dutch and Gaelic, while Laura screamed for Cameron to stop. But he raised his sword one last time and thrust it through the merchant's heart. Laura collapsed to the ground sobbing. Cameron picked her up and took her to her bedchamber in the castle, but she would not rest. She howled in anguish all through the night.

In the morning, a messenger was sent to fetch Lord Lyon home. The merchant's body was laid out in the castle's chapel, and he was buried in the kirkyard at Glamis, with his attendants and a sobbing Laura the only mourners. After the burial, his attendants headed for home, fearful and full of regret.

When Lord Lyon arrived, he barely recognised his daughter. Since the merchant's death, she had not slept a moment or eaten a bite of food, and her black hair was turning grey. All she could speak of was the horrible sight she had seen below the walnut tree. After that night, she lived half a life at best. Laura shrank into herself, shunning company and spending her days quietly pacing the corridors. For three years she lived like this, until word came that Donald Cameron had been killed in a battle against a rival clan.

Laura thought that, with Cameron dead too, she could begin to move on from that night. She asked her maidservant to help her to the garden, where she would look upon the walnut tree again for the first time. But as she took a few shaky steps towards the tree, Laura fell down in a dead faint. She never awoke from it.

Lady Laura was buried in the kirkyard at Glamis near the merchant's grave. But seven years later, his family requested that his bones be sent back to Amsterdam to lie in the family plot, so now they lie on opposite sides of the sea. And for years after, the garden of Glamis was spoken of not in wonder and admiration, but in pity and horror.

The Room of Skulls

The families of Ogilvy and Lindsay were bitter rivals. Sometimes the Ogilvies had the upper hand in Angus, and at other times it was the Lindsays. Whichever family was faring better would mercilessly persecute the other with attacks and sabotage. Once, when it was the Lindsays' turn to make war, they started a relentless campaign against the Ogilvies. They stormed their homes and set fire to their fields. The Ogilvies were in dire straits, but they would not surrender. Instead, the heads of the Ogilvy families came together under the cover of night. They made their way to Glamis Castle, where the earl had no loyalty to either side, and they begged him to give them shelter until the Lindsays grew tired of their attacks.

'Very well,' said Earl Glamis. 'You may come in.' But, while he had no loyalty to either family, he had no sympathy for any of them either. He was tired of the two families' fighting. Earl Glamis showed the Ogilvies to a room, where he said they would be safe behind the castle's thick stone walls. He told them to remain there until the coast was clear. Then he locked the heavy oak door behind him – and tossed the key into a well in the castle grounds. Glamis told his men to build another wall of stone in front of the door, as if there had never been a room there, and to ignore the shouts and cries of hunger coming from within.

The room was never opened again. Somewhere within the walls of Glamis Castle, there still lie the skeletons of the Ogilvies who came seeking shelter. The story of the betrayal was passed down as a family secret from earl to earl in horrified whispers over the years, but as is the way with stories, it found its way out into the world in the end.

LADY JANET DOUGLAS

The Douglas family were out of favour with King James V. This came about because Sir George Douglas fought alongside James in the first battle the young king ever went out in. James was just a lad and not keen on the idea of fighting. He was reluctant to get onto the field of battle, and even more reluctant to stay there once he was in the thick of it. Douglas spotted his terror.

'I know what you fear, Your Majesty,' he said, 'but there's no need to worry. Trust me, if your enemies get hold of you on one side and we have you on the other, we'll tear you in two before we surrender you.'

This was very much not what James wanted to hear. He bore a grudge against George Douglas and his entire clan for years after. He was determined that no Douglas would find favour in Scotland as long as he reigned.

So King James was not pleased when he heard that Lord Glamis had chosen young Janet Douglas as his wife, and she had given him a fine heir. This happiness at Glamis did not last long, for Lord Glamis became ill and died not long after the birth of his heir, leaving Janet to raise their son alone. But she was more than equal to the task. Janet was popular with the people of Strathmore. She had little patience for most of the trappings of noble life, and she spent a lot of time in the village. She was always interested to hear what was going on in the cottages and fields, and if anyone was ill or out of work, she was generous with her charity. Janet might have been the only genuinely popular noble in Scotland. And King James resented her popularity far more than he resented her power. He decided that he would find a way to ruin her name, and he knew exactly how to do it.

King James sent his courtiers out with the message that Lady Janet of Glamis was a witch. They said that she had been overheard whispering with Satan, making plans to poison the king himself. The rumours flew like sparks from a fire, and soon everyone was gossiping about how Janet planned to use her witchcraft to bring the Douglas family to the throne of Scotland.

Janet carried on with her life and ignored the rumours as best she could. But one day, when she was going about her visits in the village of Glamis, the king's horsemen burst through the doors of the cottage she was in. They grabbed Janet and tied her hands with ropes and dragged her out to their coach. Her son, who was still only about twelve years old, had been seized from his lessons at the castle too. The two of them were driven down to Edinburgh, where a show trial was set up and waiting for Janet.

The court in Parliament House was packed out, with the great and good from all corners of Scotland come to see Lady Janet's downfall. They were restless in their seats, itching to see her blood, but Janet stood calm and quiet. They asked her if she was a witch, if she had conspired against the king. She was calm and solemn as she denied all of their accusations.

Then the guards brought her son in as a witness. They asked the boy if he had ever seen his mother at her business of witchcraft.

'No, no!' he sobbed. 'She didn't do it.'

King James gave the nod. The guards brought forth the iron thumbscrews and boots and fixed them around Janet's hands and feet.

'Confess your crime and we will release you.'

'I am innocent,' she said again. The guards tightened the screws until her bones cracked and blood trickled onto the courtroom floor, but she sat quietly. Her son could bear the sight no longer. He tore himself from the guards' grip and ran across the courtroom. He flung himself at Janet's knee, sobbing into her skirts.

'Very well,' said the judge. 'I see the boy is involved with this plot too. Let us see if we can get a confession from him.'

The guards unscrewed the torture tools from Janet and began to fasten them around the hands and feet of her son. Still he would not betray his mother, though his face was white from the pain. But as she heard her son's bones begin to splinter, Janet cried out.

'I confess! I confess! You can have me, but for God's sake let him go!'

Well, King James's men were ready for that. Within hours, a bonfire was built around a stake at the top of Castle Hill, and the guards stood assembled with their flaming torches in hand as Lady Janet was carried up, her bones too broken to walk, and tied to the stake. And even as the flames engulfed her, she said nothing more, her face staying perfectly composed. It was said that the crowd who looked on, usually so eager with boos and hissing for the downfall of a witch, stayed silent too, and left early as if they did not quite know what to make of this execution.

But Janet was remembered at Glamis, and it seems that she remembered Glamis as well, perhaps returning from time to time to see her son grow up. To this day, people sometimes see the pale grey shape of a woman flitting around the castle, and to let Janet know that her spirit is still welcome, a chair is kept aside for the Grey Lady in the chapel.

The Monster

Legend has it that the most notorious episode in Glamis's history began on 21 October 1821. That day, Lady Charlotte Bowes-Lyon of Glamis gave birth to her first child, a son. The birth of an heir should have been a joyous occasion for the family. But Charlotte and her husband were horrified by the sight of their baby. The child, whom they named Thomas, was healthy, but he was physically disfigured. They were certain that a child who looked like this could not grow up to take on the earldom. When the midwife left the parents alone with their baby, they made a decision. It would have been better for all involved, they thought, if their son had died at birth. But he was still their son. They decided the only way to save the earldom, and the reputation of their family, was to announce that Thomas had indeed died. They would bring him up out of sight of all but a few of their most trusted servants, and to all the world it would be as if the heir of Glamis had not lived a full day. The midwife was surprised to hear the death announcement. She had left the couple with a healthy, if unusual, child. But who was she to question the Lord and Lady of Glamis?

Thomas was raised in a room hidden away in the depths of the castle, along a dark corridor. It was clear that his mind was sharp, although his short and twisted limbs and barrel chest had earned him a life of exile. In time, to their relief, the lord and lady had more children, children they were not ashamed to admit to. The earldom of Glamis could continue in the way they wanted it to. But as it became clear that Thomas still had a long life ahead of him, Lord Glamis realised he would have to let his second son in on the story.

He was a carefree young man, drinking and joking as the heirs of wealthy families tend to do. But on the evening of his twenty-first birthday, when his father took him aside at dinner and led him along the dark corridor to meet his elder brother, the young earl became a solemn and sober man overnight. All who knew him noticed the change. But he would not give a hint of what had caused it. The whole family knew there was a secret – there was no hiding that. But what it was, the earl never said. One night, his wife, seeing the worry in his face, begged him to share the burden.

'Oh, my dear,' he said. 'I can never do that. And it is just as well, for if you knew my secret, you could never know happiness again either. Please never mention the subject again.'

Thomas's family, if they ever spoke of him, called him 'The Monster'. Apart from Lord Glamis and his eldest son, the only one trusted with the full story was the factor, and it was the factor of Glamis who spent the most time with Thomas. On top of the usual duties of running the estate, it was the factor who brought Thomas food, and who took him out for his exercise, walking with him around the balconies of the castle when it was dark and they were unlikely to be seen. But sometimes, sleepless servants caught sight of a strange shape walking beside the factor, silhouetted in the dark. Perhaps Thomas was angry at being denied his place in the world, and who could blame him? But whatever the factor knew of him, it made him fearful to spend a night in the castle. One winter, when the castle was happed in snowdrifts, he insisted the servants dig a tunnel along the mile back to his cottage, rather than take a spare room for the night.

And though the earls were wary of overnight guests, they had to have strangers in the house sometimes. When the floors needed to be repaired in the 1860s, one of the workmen was looking for damaged areas and decided to check on the other side of a door leading off an upstairs hall. Looking in, he saw a long, dark corridor – and at the end of it, a pair of eyes met his, staring from something or someone he could hardly describe. When he quietly mentioned this to the clerk of works, he was met with silence. At the end of the day, the earl himself came down to see him. There was a good life to be had in Australia these days for a strong young man with a family, he said, and he'd be happy to pay the passage and a bit extra in exchange for his good work that day. The workman understood exactly the deal, or the threat, he was being offered.

The mystery went on for almost a century, and Victorian society buzzed with rumours about what could possibly be hidden at Glamis Castle. But the family kept a strict silence. It was only ninety years after Thomas's birth, when the then earl began to relax his tight grip on who was permitted to enter parts of the castle, that people suspected the secret – whatever it was – was gone. Perhaps Thomas had finally run out his long and lonely life, after almost a century spent hidden in the shadows. And perhaps the only thing which gave him the strength to survive that long was the knowledge of how deeply his very existence disturbed his heartless family.

GHOSTS OF GLAMIS

There are a host of ghouls and spirits said to be lurking around the castle. Some of their stories are here, but there are yet more whose origins have been lost, including a tongueless woman who wanders the grounds pointing to her mutilated face, and a suit of armour which moves of its own accord and sometimes wanders into sleeping folks' bedrooms.

Jack the Runner

The grounds of Glamis are almost as haunted as the castle itself. One ghost speeds across the grass, a dark sprinting shape known as Jack the Runner. His story is the most horrific of all Glamis's legends.

In the seventeenth century, when the elite of Scotland were making fortunes on the back of the Atlantic slave trade, sometimes they would bring a favourite one of the people they enslaved home with them. It became quite fashionable to have a Black servant in big houses and castles. And such a young man, who had been given Jack as his slave name, was brought to Glamis by one of the earl's friends, who was returning to Scotland from the plantation he ran in the Caribbean.

On this visit to Glamis, the earl threw a grand lunch for his visitor, and the assembled company drank and talked and joked. After their meal, they spoke about what a shame it was they didn't have a hunt to go on. A bit of sport would be just the thing, Glamis had the best hunting dogs. They just needed a fox. But the plantation owner had a suggestion. His slaves were all good runners, he said. 'Why don't we hunt Jack here?'

So Earl Glamis and his friends got the dogs from the kennels, and set them after the poor man, who was racing in mortal fear among the castle grounds while the nobles watched on and laughed. To add to their enjoyment, they brought out lances and occasionally threw one at Jack, watching as he tried to dodge their spears as well as the dogs. He ran for hours, battered and bleeding, but the dogs overtook him eventually. He was torn to pieces.

Now, the ghost of 'Jack the Runner', as he is known, still runs the grounds of Glamis, and his unearthly shrieks of agony have been heard echoing in the night.

The Page Boy

Another Black slave who was brought to Glamis was just a child, a young boy, only about six years old. He had been singled out as a pretty child on the plantations, and his masters thought that he was young enough to be trained as a good domestic servant. So he was brought to Scotland and was given as a gift to Lady Glamis, who was delighted with her new page boy.

Like any child would, he got distracted when being asked to wait quietly while the lady dressed for dinner or spoke at length to a visiting guest. He would run off to explore corners of the castle, or excitedly follow the flight of a bird in the grounds. Lady Glamis lost patience with this. He would need to be trained out of it. One day, she told him he must stop flitting about and learn to sit still. She ordered him to sit on a stone step in the corner of one room and be very quiet until she told him he could move. The boy did as he was told. He sat on the cold stone and was very still, and very quiet.

Lady Glamis went about her day, and she forgot to come back and check on her page. In fact, she wasn't sure how many days later it was when she suddenly remembered. She assumed he must have eventually got up and gone to bed – but when she returned to the room, the little child was still there, dead and stiff with cold.

Visitors to Glamis often trip up in the room where he died, as if a little boy was running about and getting under their feet.

The Barrel

One of the ghosts of Glamis is not a person at all. Maids who worked in the castle soon learned to be wary of a huge barrel which stood at the top of one of the main staircases. Every time a maid began work at Glamis, inevitably the day would come when she was asked to clean the stairs for the first time. No matter whether she began mopping from the top or the bottom of the long staircase, when she reached the middle of the stairs, she would hear a great ominous creaking and rattling, and look up to see the barrel had tipped over and was hurtling down towards her. Running for the bottom of the stairs, she would glance over her shoulder as she made for safety ... only to see the barrel had stopped its chase and had returned to its place at the top of the stairs. Every so often, the barrel would give chase to more experienced workers to keep them on their toes, but without fail it tormented every new girl who started there.

4

COAST AND RIVER

Angus's miles of coastline carry stories of comings and goings, whalers and fishermen, lighthouses and Vikings. North of Arbroath, the coast develops into red sandstone cliffs famous for their dramatic shapes, which thousands of centuries of waves have carved from the land. The place names along this stretch of coast hint at long-lost seafaring tales, with spots named the Mariner's Grave, the Deil's Heid and the Mermaid's Kirk. But many legends of Angus's seas and rivers have come down to us, and here are some of the best and strangest.

THE BATTLE OF BARRY

In the year 1010, King Sueno of Denmark and his Viking army had their sights set on Scotland. Most of England had already fallen to their attacks, but the Scots had fought them off so far. Sueno was determined to try again. He called his best general to his court, a huge, towering man by the name of Camus, and told him to lead a charge on Scotland. Camus planned to attack from the east.

A fleet of longships set sail from Denmark and made for the white sands of Lunan Bay. Hundreds of Viking warriors rushed ashore, killing everyone they saw, and were thundering towards Montrose before anyone could carry word ahead of them. They sacked the town there and then made their way inland. When they came to Brechin they burned its houses to the ground and claimed victory there too.

But King Malcolm of Scotland had been expecting an attack soon, and he quickly assembled an army at Dundee. Word got to

General Camus at Brechin that the Scots would be coming for them. He told the Vikings to march south and meet the Scots head on.

As the Scots headed north through the parish of Barry, they came to the southern bank of the Lochty Burn. The Vikings, heading south, reached the northern bank at the same time. They fought a long and bitter battle across the burn that raged for days and nights. The news spread around the land as folk called to each other:

Lochty, Lochty is reid, reid, reid,
For it has run three days wi bluid.

After days of fighting, Camus was growing tired, and he was losing men left and right. He had underestimated the army from Dundee. Camus thought that if he stayed in the field of battle much longer, it would be the end of him. He was no coward, but he knew that if he survived, he had the skills to plan another attack for King Sueno. If he died, the Viking army would be without its best leader. So he fled, and ran towards the hills by Monikie. But King Malcolm saw the giant man go. Malcolm called for his most trusted warrior, Robert de Keith, and the two set off after Camus. They caught up with him at Downie Brae. Camus drew his sword and faced up to them. He was big, but Robert was quicker, and he drew his sword and slashed it up towards Camus's head before he could get a blow in. The Viking fell down dead.

King Malcolm looked down at Camus's body on the ground, and he bent down to dip his fingers into the blood that streamed from his head. He ran them down Robert de Keith's shield to signify that he had been the one to slay Camus and save Scotland from Viking rule. Since then, the Keith family shield has had shown three red stripes in memory of that day. They buried General Camus where he fell, and to commemorate his death and the Scots' victory, a great cross was raised on the spot – the Camus Cross, which still stands at Monikie.

The Lochty Burn today runs through the small seaside town of Carnoustie. The town is well known for its crows – the black birds seem to be everywhere. Even the name Carnoustie is said to come from 'craw's nestie', and they appear on the town's crest. They are said to have been in the area since the days of the Battle of Barry. When the Norsemen's gods heard that their best warrior had been slain by the Scots, they called up a huge flock of black crows and sent it down to ravage the land where he was killed. It is the descendants of this curse of crows who still hop around the pavements of Carnoustie.

The Giant and the Dwarf

Above Lunan Bay stands the ruin of Redcastle, built from a distinctive red stone which gave the fortress its name. Redcastle was built in the days of the Vikings to defend Lunan Bay from invasions. A nobleman named Walter de Barclay lived there, ready to lead the defence if longships were sighted. King William the Lion would often visit him to see how things were on the coast, and Walter was keen to impress him. He had heard that the best royal courts engaged a giant and a dwarf among their courtiers, and Walter decided that Redcastle should be no different.

On his quest, Walter de Barclay travelled to Sweden, to pay a visit to the royal court there. He arrived at midsummer-time, when people celebrated the long days with a great festival of sports and games. Walter wandered through the field, mar-velling at the many wonders on offer. He spotted a crowd gathering in a circle, and he went to see what was holding their attention. A tournament to search for the strongest man in Sweden was being held. One man who had just won a wrestling match was standing in the middle of the circle, crying out for a competitor to take him on. The man was as broad as a barrel, and nobody seemed keen. But then Walter was amazed to see a figure emerging from the crowd, rising to the challenge. A huge man walked into the circle. He had long hair and a long beard, and he towered over everyone else at the festival. He was well over nine feet tall – even his large opponent suddenly looked tiny. Walter realised he must be descended from the legendary Norse giants he had heard tales of. Then he spotted the giant was not alone. On his shoulder there sat a man who was as small as he was huge, a dwarf who would not have come up to his friend's knee.

'My name is Daniel Cajanus,' said the giant to his opponent, and held out his hand to shake. But when the man took hold of it, Daniel lifted him up by his arm, whirled him once around his head, and threw him clean over the heads of the crowd, where he came crashing down into a nearby bush. The giant invited the crowd to step forward if anyone wanted to challenge him. They all stood still in their stunned silence.

Walter kept an eye on Daniel Cajanus as he moved through the festival, an easy task given he was head and shoulders above anyone else in the crowd. Once Daniel had taken the crown as the strongest man, his small companion – whose name was Licinius Calvus – entered the competitions for philosophical debate and he too wiped the floor with his opponents. Walter de Barclay was enchanted by the pair of them, and he was determined to see if he could bring them back to Scotland to join him at the court of Redcastle. With their combination of strength and brains, surely no invasion could challenge them – and King William would be so impressed. He asked around and heard that Daniel was descended from Goliath himself, and that Licinius was well known as a poet and speaker in his native Greece, but he had ended up in Sweden after being kidnapped in a Viking raid. He could speak countless languages, and no one had ever found a mathematical problem he couldn't solve. The two were now such close friends they were inseparable, and Daniel would do anything Licinius asked him.

At the end of the festival, Sir Walter offered Daniel and Licinius a handsome wage to come back with him to Redcastle, and they both agreed. So the three men journeyed back across the sea together, and Walter instructed his court to treat them as guests of honour. A huge dinner was held to introduce them to the Scottish nobility. When Daniel walked into the hall carrying a large silver dish, everyone gasped. When he laid the dish on the table and removed its domed cover, there stood little Licinius. The nobility were most impressed, and only grew more so over the course of the evening. Soon the two of them were famed throughout Scotland, and for years they lived at Redcastle and defended the shores of Lunan Bay from invasions.

But one night, Licinius was looking from the window of Redcastle when he saw twelve longships making for the shore. He quickly woke Daniel and Sir Walter. Along with all their men, Walter and Daniel headed for the beach with their swords and bows and arrows. Daniel led the charge fearlessly, as he always did, picking the Vikings up and hurling them back into the sea. Their ships were driven into retreat. But as they headed away, one of the Vikings took up his crossbow and fired one last shot towards Lunan Beach. It hit Daniel Cajanus in his chest, and the giant collapsed, staining the white sands red with his blood. He was dead.

His friend's death broke poor Licinius' heart in two, and he too died the next day of his sorrow. Daniel and Licinius were buried side by side at Redcastle. It is said that centuries later, a gigantic coffin and a tiny one were uncovered by workmen digging a foundation for a gate on land near the castle.

The Inchcape Rock

Just west of Aberbrothock, as the town of Arbroath was known in those days, was the estate of Kelly. The Lord of Kelly had one beautiful daughter, whose name was Ellen. When she grew into a young woman, her father was very concerned with finding her a suitable marriage match, but Ellen was in love with a young shepherd named Henry, who worked on her father's land. She would consider no other. But Lord Kelly made life very difficult for them. He would constantly make disparaging remarks about Henry, and it was plain to him that his potential father-in-law did not want him around.

When Lord Kelly was summoned to go and fight on behalf of the King of Scotland, Henry saw his chance to prove his worth. He signed up to the army too, and he swore to protect Kelly with his life. The two of them went away to the war, leaving Ellen alone.

After a few months, a letter arrived at Kelly which broke Ellen's heart in three. Her father and her love had both been lost in battle. She sobbed for three days, and she vowed to give up all earthly desires, since she could bear the grief of them no more. So she went to the Abbey of Aberbrothock, and she begged the abbess to let her enter the convent there.

'Well,' said the abbess, 'you are young, and you have suffered more than you should have to at your age. My counsel to you is to wait a year, and if your feelings have not changed, you can join the convent then.'

Ellen passed the year in near silence. She was certain there was no worldly life for her now. On the morning that she was to take her oath to God, and to Thomas Becket to whom the abbey is dedicated, she walked into the red sandstone building, ready to don her nun's robes. The monks' choir were gathered, singing hymns, and there were flowers laid out to decorate the hall. As she prepared to begin her vows, Ellen's eye caught someone watching. And she fainted dead away.

When she awoke, Ellen realised she had not been dreaming. Henry was back! He had been captured by the English army, but he had escaped, and walked all the way back to Aberbrothock by himself. She never spoke her nun's vows. Instead, before the day was out, she and Henry were exchanging their marriage vows.

Ellen and Henry had one wonderful month of happiness together. Henry had a year left to serve in the army, so he had to set off back to Edinburgh to see that out. But it was uneventful, and as Henry stepped onto the boat in Leith to return home, he was filled with joy at the prospect of settling down with Ellen for good. But it was a winter's night, and the sea was rough and angry. The waves were as high as mountains, and the boat flew from side to side. The treacherous Inchcape Rock, eleven miles from Arbroath, lurks just below the waves at high tide. The wind drove their ship straight into it and smashed her hull to pieces.

Poor Ellen's heart was broken all over again. It was more than she could bear. He never even got to meet the son who she had given birth to while he was away. The second mourning made her gravely ill, and she knew she had to arrange for her son, little Henry, to be looked after. So she went to the abbot and she bequeathed the abbey all her land and inheritance in exchange for a safe home for her little boy. And soon after, Ellen was dead.

Young Henry grew up among the monks in the abbey. Knowing the sad tale of his father's life, he chose a life of quiet contemplation over adventure. He dedicated his life to the service of God and St Thomas Becket, and in time he became the abbot himself. All his life, his thoughts returned to the Inchcape Rock, how it had stopped him from knowing his parents and had taken countless other lives in the years since. He decided that his great service to the world would be to protect anyone he could from the same fate. So he took a boat right out to the edge of the rock, loaded with materials. Day after day he returned at low tide, working long into the winter. Some say the spirit of St Thomas Becket himself came down to help, and it was on

29 December, Becket's feast day, that he completed it. Now there stood a bell on the Inchcape Rock, perfectly positioned so that the higher the waves crashed, the louder it would ring. The bell would warn ships that they were approaching the rock, and they could steer their course away before it was too late. In time, the rock itself became known as the Bell Rock. Sailors far and wide applauded the abbot's work.

Almost all sailors.

One of the most notorious pirates on Europe's seas in those days was a Dutchman by the name of Ralph Vandergroot, known as Ralph the Rover. His route home from one voyage of plunder took him past the Bell Rock. When he passed, low tide had exposed the rock. He steered his ship alongside and stepped onto the rock to take a closer look at the bell. It was good metal. He'd get a good price for it, and what of the shipwrecks? It was of no concern to a sailor of his quality, and the rest got what they deserved. Vandergroot undid the bell from its moorings and bundled it onto his ship.

Vandergroot's second in command, Jan Hanson, was not frightened by much. But when he saw what his captain had done, he grew pale.

'You've gone too far this time,' he said. 'That is an ill deed and it will bring nothing but ill luck.'

Vandergroot sneered.

'Don't be such a superstitious fool! I'll have none of that nonsense on my ship.'

'Then I will not stay on your ship. Put the bell back or put me to shore at Arbroath.'

Vandergroot was furious.

'Leaving the ship, eh, you traitor? Very well.' And he dived forwards and pushed Hanson into the sea.

Like most sailors in those days, Hanson could not swim. He floundered in the waves, his head sinking then rising again. He raised his head one last time and stared Vandergroot dead in the eye.

'You'll see me again,' he spat. And then he sank.

The Rover sailed on, and he paid no mind to the threat. In fact, when he got home to Amsterdam he hung the Inchcape Bell in his own garden, as a trophy of his adventures. But a year or so later, another voyage brought him back to Scottish seas. It was the depths of winter. In fact, it was 29 December,

St Thomas Becket's Day. He paid no mind to that either, but his crew were beginning to worry. They knew the story of how their captain had stolen the bell, and the clouds were gathering dark around the horizon. Thunder began to crack. Rain poured down in sheets and lightning lit up the sky. In the distance they could make out the lights of Arbroath, the round O window of the abbey lit like a beacon. But they could not see enough to tell where they were, or where the rock was.

As Vandergroot and his crew struggled to keep the ship upright, there was a sudden flash of blue lightning. There, standing on the deck, dripping in water and with seaweed tangled in his hair, was the ghost of Jan Hanson. The ghost let out a shrieking laugh that sounded like he was the storm itself.

'Vandergroot, you will sleep with me this night!' As the ghost cried these words, the crew were thrown to the deck. Their ship had hit the Inchcape Rock, and was splintering into pieces. There was nothing more they could do.

At that same moment in Amsterdam, Vandergroot's wife was quietly enjoying a winter's night with a few friends. The night was calm, so when she heard the bell in the garden toll, she was surprised. When the company ventured out to see what had caused it to ring, they were met with the sight of Jan Hanson's ghost, sodden and dripping seaweed, tolling the bell over and over.

TAM TYRIE THE PIPER

Tam Tyrie was the best piper in Arbroath, and he was invited to every event for miles around in the hopes that he would bring his pipes and share a few tunes, which he always did. Tam and his wife and their wee dog were familiar faces up and down the coast.

On one winter's night, they had been at a wedding a fair bit out of town, out Auchmithie way, and after the singing and the

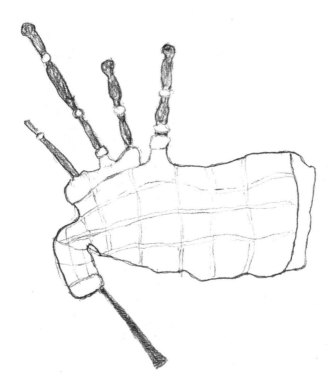

dancing and the drinking was finished, they made their way
back along the path which runs down the coast by the side of
the red sandstone cliffs. The rain was beginning to lash down,
and a strong wind was buffeting Tam, his wife and his dog as
they forged onwards. But the wind grew and grew, and as they
came towards Carlingheugh Bay they became afraid that they
would be blown into the sea. They knew there was a cave down
below the cliffs they could take shelter in, so they picked their
way down the steep path to the shore to wait out the storm.
When they came to the mouth of the cave, the wee dog growled
and bristled, but in they went.

And after that – well, the story is a mystery.

But next morning at dawn, folk at the farm of Dickmontlaw, a mile or two inland from Carlingheugh Bay, heard the unmistakeable skirl of Tam Tyrie's pipes. The sound was distant and eerie, coming from far beneath their feet. They stamped their feet and thumped their fists on the ground, hoping Tam would hear them and follow them back towards the sea. But the music drifted away. Later, they heard another sound, an echo of Tam's wife singing a sad lament as she too wandered the depths below. The folk of Dickmontlaw were haunted by this music for two or three days, and each day they tried to make themselves heard below. And then the music stopped coming. The silence was worse.

No one knows what became of Tam Tyrie and his wife in that cave. But a few days after Tam's pipes went silent, a fisherman down by the bay spotted a strange creature on the rocks, and he went over to investigate. It took him a while, but eventually he recognised Tam Tyrie's wee dog – quaking and shivering, and completely bald. Every scrap of hair was melted clean away from its body.

For good reason, the cave is now known as the Forbidden Cave, and few have dared to explore its depths since then.

The Shore Sailor

The town of Broughty Ferry, now encompassed by the expanding city of Dundee, was once a bustling fishing village. There was once a young lad who grew up there who dreamed of going to sea and making his fortune as a sailor. He couldn't wait to get on board his first boat. His dream was to work his way up from the small fishing boats his father knew, learning the ropes and moving on to the big clipper ships which set sail from Dundee to places all around the world. But the boy's dreams were dashed when he discovered that he could barely set foot aboard a boat without being overcome by the most terrible seasickness. He was determined to get past it. Day after day he spent the whole trip clinging to the deck, moaning and clutching his stomach. He could barely stand, let alone fish. One day, the captain had to tell him not to come back in the morning.

The young man was devastated. He had never wanted any life for himself but one on the sea, and now the sea did not want him. Heartbroken, he hid himself away in daydreams, and spent more and more time in the taverns by the shore. He regaled anyone who would listen with tales of adventures on the high seas, in which he was cast as the hero. He told folk he had saved the queen's ships from pirates, found safe passage through storms, and discovered islands never seen before by human eyes. He even began to wear the traditional clothes of a seafarer, the blue jacket and gold earring. Everyone who listened to him knew fine that he'd barely made it to Fife, but they hadn't the heart to tell him so. He was known to all as the Shore Sailor.

One stormy winter's night, a group of strangers came into Broughty Ferry harbour on an unfamiliar boat. They were unfriendly and wouldn't say why they were there, so most of the locals gave them a wide berth. But the Shore Sailor loved a new audience, and they plied him with whisky all night as he told his stories. As he told them about his victories at sea, they thought that he must have plenty of gold and jewels in his pockets if all that was true. So when the pub closed and the Shore Sailor stumbled off into the night, they followed him. Once they were in darkness, out of the glow of the street lamps, they hurried behind him and stabbed him in the back. They greedily rifled through his pockets. Of course, he had nothing. The only thing of any value was the gold earring he wore, so they cut it from his ear and ran back to their boat before they were discovered.

The body of the poor Shore Sailor was discovered in the morning. He had no family, and the robbers had taken the only thing that could have paid for his burial, so he lies in a pauper's grave in the old Broughty Ferry kirkyard with no stone to remember him by. But if you are walking along the shore on a winter's night, a man in old-fashioned sailor's clothing might fall into step with you and ask if you want to hear a story.

THE GANNOCHY BRIDGE

There was once a wealthy farmer named James Black whose land was at Gannochy, just outside Edzell by the banks of the River North Esk. The North Esk at this point was a fast and dangerous river to ford, and over the years many travellers had been swept away by the torrents in bad weather. Then came the worst winter anyone could remember. In the dark and the rain and the sleet, the deaths were coming faster than ever.

The folk of Edzell and Gannochy knew that a bridge was what was needed. But bridges are expensive, and they needed to find someone with a bit of money. Eventually, thoughts turned to James Black. The rumour was that he had a good bit of money saved up, and he had no family of his own to pass it down to. He was known to be a cautious and reticent man where money was concerned, though, and might not be convinced if they just asked him. But one of James's neighbours came up with a bright idea to shift his mind.

In the dead of night, the neighbour took a clean white sheet from his bed and wrapped it around himself, making a hood to hide his face. Then he tiptoed out of his house and quietly opened James Black's front door, creeping up the stairs to the bedroom. Standing at the bottom of James's bed, he let out a high mournful howl. When the farmer jolted awake all he could see was the apparition, shrouded in white, glowering down at him.

'I am the spirit of the last man to drown in the Esk,' it said, in a low voice. 'I cannot rest until the crossing is made safe. I beg you to build a bridge and save your kinfolk from my fate!'

And then it birled round in a sweep of winding sheet and was gone.

James Black was unsettled, but he said nothing the following day. But the next night, his spirit visitor came once more, and pleaded with him to see that a bridge was built. Black went out and stood on the banks of the river, looking at the current and the shore, for a long time that afternoon. But still he said nothing to the community. That night, the ghost visited him a third time.

'I still cannot rest,' it said. 'Come with me and I will show you where to build the foundations.' And the farmer followed the ghost downstairs in his nightgown, out into the cold night, towards the river. It reached out a hand shrouded in white and pointed to a spot where the river narrowed a little and ran through a deep gorge.

'Build there, James Black, and see that you do.'

And as soon as the sun was up the next morning, Black hired the best mason in Angus to come and lay the foundations for a bridge at Gannochy. He paid for every penny of the construction, and he helped to lay the stones himself as well, carving and placing the parapets with his own hands. When he died, he left money to maintain the bridge for years into the future. James Black's bridge, with a few adjustments, still stands to this day – and the ghost of Gannochy seems to have been laid to rest, too.

STORMY GRAIN

Further downstream on the North Esk there is another bridge with a story to tell. The North Esk river runs close to the northern border of Angus, reaching the sea between Montrose and St Cyrus. Near Montrose is the House of Dun, which was home to the Erskine family.

One night, Erskine of Dun had a dream. As he slept, a voice said very clearly, 'Your life's work is to build a bridge where three waters meet in one. You must do this, or you will be miserable until the day you die.'

When Erskine woke he was uneasy, because the voice felt very real, and he had no doubt its words were true. But he had no idea where three waters met in one. He looked at maps of seas and rivers, but he could not figure it out.

One day Erskine was walking along the North Esk, wondering whether he would ever find his purpose, when he met an old woman washing clothes in the river. He saw the water was white and wild in the stretch where she was working, and he stopped to ask her why this part of the river was so rough.

'This is Stormy Grain,' she said. 'It's where the three streams meet in the North Esk.'

Erskine knew this was his place. But the water was high and the flow was fast, and the mud on the riverbank was not fast. It would be a hard place to build a bridge. But he set about it anyway, getting a cart to bring stones up to Stormy Grain for the foundations. He spent all the next day from dawn till dusk putting them in place. But in the night a heavy rain came and washed them into the river. When he arrived to the wreckage the following morning, he rescued his stones from the river and began again. That night it rained once more, heavier than before, and with a strong wind to go with it too. This was how it went all Erskine's first week of building, he spent the day redoing the work the elements had destroyed overnight.

He began to feel like he would never build the bridge, and that meant he was doomed to a life of misery. On the seventh day, he could not summon the energy to get out of bed. He lay staring at the white ceiling of his bedroom, thinking about how cruel fate had been to him. As he lay there, he saw a little spider creeping across the ceiling. It began to spin a web in the corner of the room. After a while, the thread failed and it went tumbling to the floor. But a few seconds later the spider had scuttled back up the wall and was trying again. Once more the thread failed. And once more the spider returned.

Erskine watched the little creature fall and climb back up, time after time. On its seventh attempt, the thread held fast, and soon a fine web was growing across the corner of the room. He looked at the spider and thought he had to give the bridge one more try. Erskine leapt out of bed and threw on his boots and coat, and he made his way back to the riverbank. With new determination, he laid once again the foundations for the bridge. This time, the night was dry, and when he returned the next day the foundations were still in place. Erskine finished building the bridge at Stormy Grain, and it remains exactly where he built it to this day.

Kelpie Tales

Many of Angus's rivers are home to a kelpie. The kelpie is an ancient and powerful creature, whose true form is that of a huge dark water-horse, with dripping seaweed for hair. They might shapeshift into the guise of a friendlier horse, or even a human being, to lure you into their watery homes. Kelpies are renowned for their extraordinary strength, which is far greater than that of a normal horse. This sometimes tempts people to use magic to harness kelpies for their own ends, but it is a tactic which rarely ends well.

The Kelpie of St Vigeans

One such kelpie lived by the village of St Vigeans, which lies near Arbroath on the Brothock Water. The Church of St Vigeans sits at the top of a steep mound, one of those hills that seems to come out of nowhere. Its slopes are now covered with generations of gravestones. Legend has it that the mound, sturdy as it looks, sits atop a deep, dark loch, which connects underground to the Brothock Water. And this loch was home to a kelpie.

In the days of the Picts, a holy man came to convert the people of Arbroath to Christianity. He had his work cut out for him, and he knew that if he was going to succeed, he would need a church. The only place which would do was on the top of the hill, above the kelpie's loch. But it was too steep for men to carry the stones to the top. So the holy man went to one of the skilled Pictish metalworkers, and got a huge bridle made up with a silver crucifix upon it, and he went down to the Brothock Water and waited for a sight of the kelpie.

When the great dark water-horse emerged from his loch, the holy man crept behind him and threw the bridle over his back. The kelpie stomped and thrashed the river into a great storm, but it was no use – the power of the cross compelled him to do man's bidding. The first thing he had the kelpie do was lay huge iron bars where the church's foundations were to be, so that any magical revenge the kelpie may try would be stopped. And the holy man piled stones onto his back and thrashed him up the hill with them, day after day, trip after trip. The kelpie cried mournfully as he worked, sighing:

Sair back and sair banes, carryin' the Kirk o Vigeans stanes!

When the church was finished, the holy man took off the bridle, and he let the kelpie go.

'You may have your kirk,' said the kelpie, 'but you may have a curse with it. If anyone takes the sacrament within its walls, the kirk and all who's in it will crumble down into my loch, and every soul in the place will drown.'

And for years, the people of St Vigeans refused to take Communion in the church. They would go through every other part of worship, but not that, for fear of the kelpie's threat. In 1736 there was a minister in post there who was a very modern-thinking man, and he was sick and tired of the pagan superstition of his people.

So one Sunday he announced, 'That's it. Next week I shall hold Communion whether you like it or not.'

The kirk was near empty the following week. But on a hillock, across the water from the church, the congregation huddled in a crowd, breath held to see whether the kelpie's words would come true. But the minister held his lonely service and there was no crack of stone, no screaming fall into the depths below. So they have taken Communion as normal at St Vigeans since then. But it may be that the kelpie still lives in the loch below the hill, biding his time and waiting for his moment.

St Vigeans is home to important Pictish symbol stones, and the horse-like creature carved on one of them might be what inspired this story. There was also once said to be a monk, by the name of Turnbull, who lived in a bare and basic room in the steeple of St Vigeans Church. He lived a happy monastic life there until one day the Devil appeared to him in the form of a rat, and since then the steeple of St Vigeans has been left empty.

Waterstone

There was a kelpie at the ford of Waterstone on the Noran Water, just east of Castle Vayne. This kelpie adored wild weather, and when storms whipped the water he was at his happiest, leaping along the riverside and overturning the rocks in the swollen water. He kicked one rock so hard one day that he left the imprint of his hoof forever embedded in its surface, known ever after as the Kelpie's Footprint. The Kelpie of Waterstone was a trickster who enjoyed seeing humans perish in the river. The ford at Waterstone is clear and often calm, so people think it is safe, but it is deeper than it looks, and hidden currents run below the surface. The kelpie would call out plaintively, feigning the voice of someone drowning, so anyone within earshot would run to the ford hoping to save them – and often fall into the depths themselves.

If someone was genuinely in trouble, this delighted the Kelpie too. He would head in the opposite direction to the drowning soul and call out: 'All the men o Waterstone, come here, come here!'

The rescuers would rush to the wrong place and, more often than not, another life was lost to the Noran Water. Tommy's Pot, a pool in the river near where the Kelpie lurks, is named for a poor wee lad who drowned there many years ago. The place name Vayne is also said to come from this sad moment, commemorating Tommy's father's sobs of 'It's a' vane!' when he realised his son could not be rescued.

These kelpies have many kinfolk in the rivers of Angus. Another water-horse was pressed into service to build the bridge of Shielhill over the South Esk. On what used to be the border between Angus and Kincardineshire, a kelpie was ill-used by the Laird of Morphie to carry the stones to build his castle. The kelpie left him with a curse too – *The Laird o Morphie'll never thrive, as lang's the Kelpie is alive*. And the River Isla is home to a Kelpie's Pool. This is a grand place to swim, but the name reminds us to be wary of the river's power.

5

THE CITY

Dundee, between the Tay and the Sidlaw Hills, is a small city with a lot of stories. It has been inhabited since prehistoric times, and the city we know today grew from a tiny walled medieval town into a crowded industrial centre known for weaving and whaling, swallowing up the village of Lochee as it grew. It can be hard to separate history from legend in Dundee. Its industries, and its attempt to recover from their decline, have brought waves of demolition and rebuilding, and stories have stepped in to fill the gaps in a dramatically changing cityscape. Many of old Dundee's buildings have gone, but the characters in these stories still walk the streets of the imagined city.

THE STRATHMARTINE DRAGON

Near Bridgefoot on the banks of the Dighty Burn, there lived a farmer with nine dutiful daughters. One Sunday morning, he told the youngest to go to the well and fetch a bucket of water for the household. Of course, she obeyed her father, and off she went. But when she got there, she was horrified. A huge dragon was coiled around the well, and it was not going to let anyone near the water. She turned to run home, but it had picked up her scent. And it was hungry. In no time at all, she had become the dragon's breakfast.

Her father wondered where she'd got to. He asked one of her older sisters to go and get her to hurry up. Soon, he was waiting on two girls. So he asked another sister, and another, and another … Whatever could these girls be getting up to? Before the

morning was out, the farmer had sent all of his daughters to meet a horrible fate at the teeth and claws of the dragon.

Eventually, the farmer decided he would have to go after them himself. And only then did he see the hulking beast curled up around the well, still licking blood from its lips. He sprinted into the village to raise the alarm.

'There's a dragon at the well!' he cried. 'A dragon! And it's eaten all of my daughters!'

The first to respond to his cries was a young man named Martin. Martin was the apprentice blacksmith, and he had been in love with the farmer's eldest daughter. He was furious. Martin grabbed the biggest hammer he could find in the smithy and ran off towards the well.

The dragon was a wee bit alarmed when it saw Martin storming towards it, waving the hammer, with his face set in determination. But not too much. This was nothing a bit of fire-breath couldn't handle … was it? Flames shot from its nose, but Martin dodged them and swiped sideways at the dragon's neck. Soon they were leading each other on a terrible chase around the hills and fields, each just escaping the other's attacks.

All the village was watching in awe, silently praying for Martin's success. But the dragon was getting the upper hand. It loomed towards Martin, narrowing its eyes, opening its huge dark jaws …

'Strike, Martin!' cried the crowd. Summoning up the last bit of his courage, Martin slammed his hammer hard into the side of the dragon's head, and ran for safety as it collapsed onto the ground. The dragon laid its head on a stone, and grumbled out a last lament as it died:

> I was tempted at Pittempton
> Draigelt at Baldragon,
> Stricken at Strikemartin,
> And killed at Martin's Stane.

Forever after, Martin's fight with the dragon has been remembered through these place names, and although the name of Strikemartin has since become Strathmartine, they are still used in Dundee to this day. The stone on which the dragon died was carved with images commemorating the battle, and can still be seen at Kirkton of Strathmartine. As for the well which the dragon guarded, this remained for hundreds of years, too. People used to come from far and wide to see it. But one farmer at Strathmartine in the Victorian era got tired of people tramping across his fields to visit the dragon's well and ruining the crops, so he covered it over with stones. Dundee still remembers the legend, though, and a statue of the dragon takes pride of place on the High Street.

COUTTIE THE DROVER

In medieval times, Dundee was kept safe from invasion by a protective wall around its boundaries. The city then was much smaller than it is now. The four 'gaits' of the town – the Overgate, Wellgate, Murraygate and Seagate – made up the most of it. The Hilltown fell outside the wall, and it was not protected by the laws of the city. Outlaws and dodgy traders made a beeline for it, and it got a reputation as a wild and dangerous place. But it was where the main road into Dundee from the north came down, and so it was still frequented by many travellers.

One of these travellers was a drover named Couttie. Couttie kept a small herd of cattle at a steading up in the Angus glens. He had been into Dundee to sell some of his cows at the market, and he made his way back up through the Hilltown, accompanied by his faithful collie. He was especially wary coming through here on the way back from a sale, knowing the place's reputation, and that the money he now had on him would be his only income for months.

As he got into his stride, a stranger wearing the humble rags of a beggar fell into pace beside him. At first, Couttie was suspicious, but the other traveller seemed safe enough, and they were probably both safer in each other's company. As they talked, Couttie noticed the man was very reluctant to give any details on his own life, but he was well versed in news and politics, and they carried on a friendly discussion about affairs of state.

The journey passed quickly this way, and Couttie and his friend grew relaxed. But when they came near the top of the hill, the little dog pricked up his ears and began to growl in fear. Before they knew what was happening, a band of armed robbers was upon them. Couttie pulled out the small knife he kept in his pocket, and tried to fend them off. He was relieved to see his friend was a good fighter, and his dog got in a fair bit of damage too. But they were hugely outnumbered by the robbers, and Couttie couldn't see a way out of this.

Just as he was on the verge of giving up, he heard his friend call out: 'Fight on, Couttie, for the face of a king is terrible!'

Couttie and the robbers came to the same realisation at once. They were not in the company of a wandering beggar, but of King James IV. There were always rumours that Scotland's king would travel anonymously to see how his people acted when they were not aware of who he was, but none of them had really believed it until now. Fearing he would have an army in reserve just out of sight, the robbers took to their heels and fled, leaving Couttie and the king to finish their journey in peace.

King James was so impressed with Couttie's bravery that day that he made him a gift of a piece of land in the centre of Dundee, and you can still find Couttie's Wynd in the heart of the city today.

WALLACE'S FIRST BATTLE

In 1288, Scotland was under English rule. King Edward I had seized control of the country and had placed English governors in every Scottish castle to enforce his will. Dundee was no different. At Dundee Castle there was a governor named Selby in place. His teenage son came with him, and was finishing his education at the High School of Dundee. Young Selby fancied following in his father's footsteps, and enjoyed lording it over his classmates, making sure no one was in any doubt about his high status. This wound up the local boys to no end. He made a particular enemy with one boy from a well-known Scots family, a lad named William Wallace, who had plenty of his own ambitions.

One Saturday, Wallace was walking near the West Port of Dundee with a few friends. He'd dressed in his best suit of green that morning, the colour of wealth and power – he wanted to make sure the folk of Dundee knew he was someone to remember. But there was young Selby, sneering as usual.

'What devil clad thee in a suit so gay, you Scots peasant? You've no right to be wearing that. Oh, and I see you have a knife – I don't think my father's given you permission for that either! You'll have to hand it over to me.'

'Hand it over, aye?' Wallace was furious. 'You'll have to come and get it!' And the two young men were soon fighting, not for the first time. But this time Wallace had had more than enough of Selby's attitude, of living under his father's rule, and he was a man of quick temper. In a rage he drew out his knife and stabbed the governor's son. Selby fell down dead. And Wallace knew he was in big trouble. He had to get out of the city as quickly as possible. Pelting off through the gate of the West Port before anyone knew what had happened, Wallace ran for his life up the Perth road. He had an uncle at Kilspindie who would shelter him. He only had to make it through the Carse of Gowrie.

It didn't take long before the full force of Governor Selby's army was on his trail. Wallace ran and ran until he reached Longforgan. There, he became so exhausted that he just had to stop for a rest. Wallace collapsed onto a large quernstone outside a cottage.

Soon, the woman who lived there noticed there was a bedraggled and exhausted looking young man on her quern-stone. She came out with a jug of milk and some bread, and asked him what sort of journey he was on.

Wallace thought about it. Most people resented the governor's rule as much as he did, so he took a chance and told her the true story.

'Oh, you must come inside if they'll be after you!' she cried. He didn't need to be asked twice. 'We'll keep you well hidden,' the woman said, and took her spare dress out from the kist. Soon, Wallace was wearing it, with a shawl arranged around his head, and doing his best to look as if he knew how to spin wool on the spindle in the corner of the room.

The sound of banging on every door in the village told them that the soldiers had arrived. They forced open doors and yelled at the inhabitants to give up any runaways they might be hiding, but got nothing but blank stares. When they burst into the cottage, they took a good look around, casting their eyes right over Wallace as he sat and span.

'Have you seen a young man pass this way?' they demanded. But the woman shook her head.

'It's just been me and my sister all day, I cannae help you there.'

And they went on their way, the sound of banging and shouting drifting off through Longforgan. Wallace stayed in the cottage until dark fell, and later, under cover of night – and the same disguise – the woman's husband led him safely to his uncle's house at Kilspindie. But that day had changed the course of his life forever. William Wallace was now an outlaw, and he would fight again many a time to oust English control of Scotland.

Descendants of the family who rescued Wallace kept the stone thought to be the one he rested on for over six hundred years, and eventually donated it to the McManus Galleries in Dundee. If this is indeed the stone, it has lasted much longer than Dundee Castle, which changed hands several times between Scotland and England in the years after Wallace's escape, and was finally destroyed in 1313 as Robert the Bruce fought to reclaim Dundee for the Scots.

THE DOCTOR AND THE CAT

At the end of the sixteenth century, there was a doctor by the name of David Kinloch who practised in Dundee. He was an expert in the human body and its ways, but his talents didn't stop there. He could speak several languages, and when he was not practising medicine, he studied the latest literature and wrote his own poetry in Latin. Patients from wealthy families from all across Scotland made their way to Dundee to seek his opinion on any illness that troubled them, for he was renowned as the best medical man in the country. Even King James VI went to be treated by Kinloch, and was so impressed with his treatment that he appointed him as his court physician. As the king got to know Kinloch better, he began to rely on the doctor's advice, not just on matters of health but of politics. Kinloch became a trusted advisor to King James.

When King James wanted to discuss a matter with the King of Spain, who better to send over as his representative than Kinloch? So the doctor put medicine aside for a while and made the journey to Europe. But these were the days of the Spanish Inquisition, and the King of Spain was suspicious of all visitors from abroad. When Kinloch came into his court, the king called him a spy, and his guards dragged him off to jail. He feared for his freedom – and his life.

Desperate for news from Scotland, or word of a potential pardon, Kinloch took to eavesdropping on the jailers as they chatted during their long shifts. But this was the only human contact that he had. He was completely alone in his cell. There was only one bright spot in these long days. A beautiful black cat was in the habit of prowling around the walls of the prison, basking in the sun in the yard. She would often sneak between the bars of the cells too, because she was guaranteed lots of attention from the lonely prisoners. The cat took a liking to Kinloch, and she would sit with him for hours while he stroked her glossy black coat.

One day, Kinloch overheard the jailers talking about the news that the Grand Inquisitor had fallen gravely ill. It sounded as if the best doctors in Spain had all been called in, and they were

at a loss for how to treat him. Kinloch called out from his cell
in Spanish.

'I'm the King of Scotland's best doctor! Let me see him – I'm
sure I could find a way to cure him!'

But the jailers just laughed. 'Doctor, eh? That's a new one!'

Kinloch knew that his fame had spread beyond Scotland.
If he could get word to the inquisitor and his doctors, they
would want his assistance, and it could just be his ticket out
of there. But how could he do that when the jailers refused to
help? He sat and stroked the black cat and plotted. As he did
so, he thought about how shiny her coat was, how healthy and
well-fed she seemed to be. This was no street moggy. This was a
wealthy family pet, and perhaps she even belonged to somebody
very high-up.

In his pocket, he had the pen and ink and physician's reference
book he never left home without. He tore a page from it and
wrote his message in the margin, explaining who, and where, he
was. Then he ripped a long strip of cloth from his shirt, and he
used it to tie the note around the cat's tail. As Kinloch watched
her leap through the window, he silently prayed the note would
find the right eyes.

That evening, the jailer came to his cell door, accompanied
by a man wearing the robes of the Inquisition. This was either
good news, or very bad news indeed.

'Are you the doctor?' the man asked. When Kinloch nodded,
the man said, 'Follow me, then. Let's hope you're as good as they
say you are.'

The man led him to the Chief Inquisitor's house, and up
to his bedchamber. The man who was feared throughout the
country lay there, looking frail and close to death. But after a
quick examination, Kinloch thought he saw what the cause
was. He wrote down a list of the herbs he would need, and
when a servant brought them in, he measured them out
exactly and mixed them with the most care he had ever taken

in his life – and he had always been a very careful man. As he waited for the inquisitor to drink the medicine he had brewed, Kinloch knew that if this didn't work, it would be the end of him for sure.

In an hour or so, the doctor was relieved to see the patient began to stir. The colour came back to his cheeks. Soon he could sit up, and in two hours he could stand. The cure had worked.

The first thing the inquisitor did was to give Kinloch back his freedom. And then he arranged for an escort to the harbour, where the doctor boarded the first ship heading back to Scotland with much rejoicing. David Kinloch returned to Dundee, and later to his family home in the Howe of Strathmore. He lived out the rest of his illustrious career there, and his grave can be found in the Howff graveyard in Dundee.

BLUIDY CLAVERS

John Graham of Claverhouse, 1st Viscount Dundee, was a man of two nicknames. To his admirers, Jacobite supporters of the Stuarts' claim to the throne, he was Bonnie Dundee – a handsome and formidable military strategist. But to his enemies, Covenanters who supported William of Orange and a Presbyterian Scotland, he was Bluidy Clavers. To them, it was as if he had been sent by the very Devil to torment them – and the story goes that perhaps that was indeed the case.

Graham's family home was at Claypotts Castle, on the banks of the Dighty. There, the Devil came to meet him one night.

'I will lead a Rising soon,' Graham said to his friend, 'and I need to ask your protection. Can you bring me a warlock's fecket?'

A warlock's fecket was a rare and dangerous thing. It was a jacket made from the skin of water-snakes, and it had to be sewn at a full March moon. A man wearing this could not be killed by gunshot, it was said, for bullets would simply slide off it like water. The Devil promised Graham he could provide this – but it would cost him his soul, and the use of Claypotts Castle when he wished. Bluidy Clavers shook hands with the Devil, and the deal was done. Auld Clootie was better than his word. When he came to deliver the warlock's fecket, he had an extra gift – a great black horse which he'd ripped by hand from its mother's womb as a foal. It had grown to be the fastest horse in the land, and it could cross any raging ford with ease.

So it was armed with the Devil's protection, and riding the Devil's horse, that the Covenanters said Graham led his men to the Battle of Killiecrankie, where he led the Jacobite charge against the government's army. His regiments of Highlanders and Irishmen were small, but they were better trained than their opponents, and determined, and they charged their enemies with ferocity. The battle was soon going in Graham's favour. But one man among the government's soldiers thought of the stories he'd heard before the battle, how Graham was protected from bullets. He unpicked a silver button from his soldier's jacket and slid this into his musket in place of a bullet. Then he waited, bracing himself against the throng, until he could see Bluidy Clavers himself on his big black horse. Carefully, he took aim, and fired.

His aim was good. The silver button shot through the snake-skin of the warlock's fecket, and pierced Graham's heart. He slid down from his horse into the mud. The Jacobite Rising was victorious that day, but Bluidy Clavers was dead.

And the Devil, for his part, has kept up his claim to Claypotts Castle. Each Hallowe'en night, he still hosts a grand party there, where demons and witches can be heard dancing and whooping in its darkened halls.

This vision of 'Bluidy Clavers' was a tenacious one in the folklore of Dundee – and Scotland – for generations. Walter Scott reintroduced

'Bonny Dundee's' side of the story into popular tradition with his song of the same name, with its rousing chorus 'it's up wi the bonnets o bonny Dundee!' The Jacobites of Angus have plenty legends from their own side of the story too, some of which are included later in the book.

THE BROONIE OF CLAYPOTTS

Not all the supernatural residents of Claypotts were as terrifying as the demons that folk said Claverhouse invited in. The castle was one of those households lucky enough to be home to a Broonie, who helped out with the chores of the house. Like most of his kin, the Broonie of Claypotts was a wee, wizened hairy creature, and he came out mostly at night. As long as somebody left out a bowl of porridge or milk for him, he would sweep the floor and clean the pots – because despite being small, Broonies are very strong, and can easily lift and scrub and work. They are very temperamental creatures, though. You should never get on the wrong side of a Broonie.

By the nineteenth century, the castle was still owned by the Claverhouse family, but they didn't live there anymore. The land around Claypotts was now the farm of Balunie, and the castle itself was being used as a very distinctive farmhouse. The Broonie was still very much at home and helping out there, making sure that Claypotts and the farm were spick and span.

But try as he might, the Broonie just couldn't keep up with the mess made by one of the farm servants. This lass could cause chaos just by standing still, and when she went about her work she caused even more. She spilled flour all over the floor when it was her turn to bake, she splashed the milk around the flagstones in the dairy when she was milking, and she left rags and dishcloths scattered around the place when she made a half-hearted attempt to clean up. The Broonie watched her and grew more and more infuriated every day.

One day, the servant was in the vegetable garden, gathering some kale for that evening's dinner. She pulled up handfuls of the kale and wandered into the house, leaving a trail of mud from her boots and lumps of earth which fell from the kale's roots. The Broonie could stand it no longer. He crept out from his hiding place and followed her into the kitchen, where he leapt up onto her back and snatched the kale from her hands. *Whack, whack, whack* – he thrashed the poor girl across the head with the kale, so hard the vegetables completely disintegrated. Then he leapt down again and stood in the doorway, by now with all the household's servants gawping at him. With these words, the Broonie cursed the house and the whole of the land it stands in:

> The Ferry and the Ferry-well,
> The Camp and the Camp-hill,
> Balmossie and Balmossie Mill,
> Burnside and Burnhill.

> The thin sowans o Drumgeith,
> The fair May o Monifieth,
> There's Gutherston and Wallaceton,
> Claypotts I'll gie my malison!

> Come I late or come I ear,
> Balunie's boards are aye bare.

And with that, the Broonie disappeared, never to be seen again. Claypotts stands empty now, so maybe he did take all the luck of the place away with him, too.

GRISSEL JAFFRAY

There was once a woman by the name of Grissel Jaffray who lived in Dundee. She came from Aberdeen originally. Her husband, James Butchard, was a brewer who made a good living, and they stayed in a house in Calendar Close, off the bustling Overgate, which in her day – the 1660s – was a fashionable part of the town. They were well known around the city, and involved in public life. Grissel and James had one son, and when he came of age he went to sea. He did well for himself there, and soon became a ship's captain of some renown. It seemed like everything in her world was as it should be.

But one November day in 1669, three of Dundee's Presbyterian ministers decided that Grissel was a witch. Perhaps it was her Quaker faith that made them do it, or perhaps they thought she held too much sway in the city. But whatever it was, the town guards came to her door, and she was dragged off to the Tolbooth to await her trial. Grissel Jaffray, a respectable and well-to-do woman, became Dundee's most infamous witch almost overnight. Stories of the magic she was accused of casting sprung up around her.

People said that, after her arrest, Grissel was held in the Tolbooth for three days and three nights. Guards were told to watch her overnight, for fear that she would make her escape by magical means. On the first night, they watched her sit quietly until dawn, and the same on the second. But on the third, worn out by lack of sleep, both the guards nodded off.

They awoke to the sight of Grissel levitating in the air, halfway up the cell wall, her hands dripping a white substance. They sprang to their feet and tore her down, and she cried out: 'Och, ye might hae let me be until I had got the sowans o Ballumbie skinned!' Sure enough, her hands were covered in the skin of the sowans, oats soaked in milk. From that day on, the sowans at Ballumbie Castle in the east of Dundee never had a proper skin.

At her trial, Grissel was quickly found guilty of witchcraft. She was sentenced to death by burning at the Seagate, where all such executions took place.

On the day of her execution, Grissel's son was steering his ship back from a voyage. He had no knowledge of his mother's fate. As he came up the Tay past Broughty Ferry, and Dundee appeared on his horizon, the wind carried a waft of smoke towards the boat. Fearing the city may be under attack, he asked the cabin boy to row ahead of them and quickly report back on the source of the fire. A little while later, the boy returned.

'They are burning the witch Grissel Jaffray,' he said.

'Turn the ship around!' the captain called. And with no further word than that, he sailed back through the mouth of the Tay and out into the ocean. He never set foot in Dundee again.

Grissel Jaffray has long been remembered in Dundee. In the Howff graveyard, there is a stone pillar which is thought of as a memorial for her, as she never got a proper gravestone. People leave little offerings, coins or tokens, in honour of her and in the hope that Grissel's spirit may help them in a time of need. Some folk also say that, if you are in the Seagate late at night or early in the morning, when the pubs have closed and the road is quiet, sometimes a plume of smoke still drifts through the night air, and the sound of distant screams can be heard on the wind.

'Grissel's Pillar' in the Howff was in fact originally placed there to mark the meeting place of the Nine Trades of Dundee committee. It was in the middle of a graveyard then, too. She is also now commemorated by mosaics of fire and water, one at either end of Peter Street, which runs between the Murraygate and the Seagate.

JAMIE MORE AND THE FAIRIES

There was once a weaver from the Hilltown of Dundee named Jamie More. Jamie loved a party. He was usually to be found in the middle of the crowd at fairs, urging his friends to have just one more drink before they went home. This was the way it was one June night, when Jamie and his workmates walked out to Longforgan to see the midsummer fair there. The other weavers left in the early evening, knowing they had a long walk back to Dundee ahead of them. But not Jamie, he would be there until the end. And he was disappointed when, around midnight, the last few fiddlers put their instruments away and prepared to go home.

Jamie started on his way back home to Dundee. It was one of those summer nights when the sky was like twilight even in the dead of night, and he still had a half bottle of whisky in his pocket for company. So when Jamie got around halfway back to the city and spotted a group of people in the distance, laughing and singing, he thought he'd found his chance for another party. As he approached them, he noticed their clothes were unusual – fine, well-made and colourful, but strangely old-fashioned. There was something a little bit different about them. But he offered them a dram, and they were glad to accept it. Before he knew it, one of them took hold of Jamie's arm, and they swept him off towards the Sidlaw Hills in a buzz of laughter and chatter. Jamie noticed they were travelling fast – eerily fast, if he'd thought about it, but he was having a good time, so he didn't.

When they came to the Sidlaws, Jamie was amazed to see the leader of the group walk up to the hillside, and as he did so, a door appeared in front of him. The door swung open and they took him down into a huge hall within the hills, lit by flaming beacons along the walls. There was a long table laden with every type of food and drink he could imagine. There were musicians with fiddles and pipes and flutes, all playing wonderful tunes he had never heard before. Jamie More had been brought to the land of the fairies, hidden away within the Sidlaw Hills. They feasted, danced, and – mostly – drank the night and most of the morning away.

And that was all that Jamie could remember. Next thing he knew, he could feel damp grass on his face and someone was calling his name. He opened his bleary eyes and dragged himself up to a seat. He saw the familiar slopes of the Law, and the chimneys of Dundee laid out in front of him.

'Oh,' he said to himself, 'the fairies must have dropped me hame.'

Jamie swore blind to his friends that this is exactly what happened to him that night. I don't think many of them believed him, but you can make up your own mind. It has been said, though, that the name of the Sidlaw Hills comes from the Gaelic word *sidhe*, meaning the fairy folk, and that they live where the cairns are dotted around the hilltops there.

THE BLACK LADY OF LOGIE

On the road between Dundee and Lochee, there once stood a beautiful mansion named Logie House, which sat on a grand estate. One of the masters of Logie was a young man named Fletcher Read. Fletcher inherited the estate from his parents, and while he was not as canny a man as his father had been, he certainly gave the folk of Lochee a lot more to gossip about. Sport, drinking and high society were Fletcher's priorities. He also had a thirst for travel, and the family had links to the East India Company.

So Fletcher took off to see the Empire, and he found himself enjoying the lavish hospitality of one of the Indian Maharajahs. As Fletcher returned to the palace again and again, the Maharajah's beautiful young daughter caught his eye. He was of the age when he ought to be looking for a wife, though settling down was far from his mind. Over the next few evenings, Fletcher worked on persuading the Maharajah that he would be a suitable husband for his daughter. He exaggerated his social standing in Scotland, and he promised over and over that he would look after his new bride carefully. 'As if she were a child in a cradle,' he said. Although the Maharajah was concerned about seeing his daughter start a new life so far away, eventually he consented to the wedding. For a time, Fletcher was delighted.

But once he returned to Logie, he soon grew tired of his exotic new wife. The princess was struggling to adjust to life at Logie, as she did not speak much Scots or English, and Fletcher showed no interest in learning to communicate with her. He spent more and more evenings out drinking and resented having to come home to her sorrowful eyes. So Fletcher had a small summerhouse built in the grounds, which he called the Cradle House, thinking back to his promise to her father with bitter humour. He sent his wife to live there, alone, with no one to talk to but one servant who took food and drink to the house for her. Weeks of neglect and homesickness drove her to distraction.

At last, the princess decided she had to try to make contact with someone – anyone – who might help her. When the servant brought her food that day, she mimed writing until he figured out that she wanted paper and a quill. He had the sense to sneak these out of the house without asking Fletcher's permission, but he could not find any ink. That night, in desperation, the princess broke a glass and cut herself, using the blood to scribble her plea for help. She folded up the note and flung it from the summerhouse window, praying it would come into the hands of someone who had the power to help her.

The next day, one of Logie's groundsmen found the note. Seeing the blood, he was horrified and suspicious, and he too

knew better than to involve Fletcher in the matter. But the princess could not write in English, and he could not read Hindustani. Though he did have a good idea where he could find someone who could. There was a convent nearby where he knew some of the nuns had spent time in India, and he rushed there at the first chance he had. He soon found a translator, and he watched the nun's shocked face as she read the letter. She told him he must take the note to the East India Company's ship in Dundee Harbour, and see that it was taken immediately to the Maharajah so he could see the fate he had consigned his daughter to.

On the very next sailing back to Dundee, there came a spy sent by the Maharajah. The spy took lodgings in Dundee and immediately began asking questions about Fletcher Read. Soon he was speaking to the servants of Logie on their afternoon off, making plans to infiltrate Logie and rescue the princess.

But in the Cradle House, the princess was cut off from the world and had no way to know her note had reached sympathetic eyes. Feeling that she had nothing to live for, she had been growing sicker by the day, and before her rescue could be completed, she was dead. Her husband shed not a tear for her.

Upon learning of his daughter's death, the Maharajah vowed he would have his revenge on Fletcher. Knowing that greed was all that motivated him, he sent a letter to Logie saying that as the bereaved husband, a huge fortune belonging to the princess was now owed to him, but he had to come back to India in order to arrange its transfer. Fletcher was on the first boat he could find. At the port, he found the Maharajah waiting for him, not with riches but with four soldiers on fine black horses. They seized him and tied a rope to each of his arms and legs, then drove their horses off to the four points of the compass. Fletcher Read was torn limb from limb.

Although Read never returned to it, the house at Logie stood for two centuries more. The people who lived in the house after those days often said it felt a sorrowful place. And sometimes, in the evenings, they would see an Indian woman wandering mournfully around the house and its gardens, a pitiful ghost who became known to all as the Black Lady of Logie.

THE COFFIN MILL

When the air in Dundee was thick with smoke and dust, and the air rang with the clacking of hundreds of looms, one of the biggest mills was the Coffin Mill on Brook Street. Its official name was Logie Works, but no one in the city called it that. Its nickname sounds eerie, but it came from the building's shape – the buildings which formed the mill were long and straight, and slanted towards each other to join at one end in a shape like a coffin's. Between the buildings lay a big yard, with a narrow iron bridge above it linking the top floors of the buildings.

In the mills, the work was hard and the days were long, and most of the workers were women. This was because the mill owners could get away with paying them less, though they'd often say it was because women's smaller and more nimble hands were better suited to operating the big machines. This meant that, in Dundee families, often the women of the house brought in the wages, while the men stayed at home – kettle bilers – or looked for jobs that weren't there, losing their work in the mills when they turned old enough to be worth a man's wage.

There was once a family like this in Dundee, who found themselves in a terrible state when the mother, who'd been the only earner, took ill and died. The father couldn't find work no matter how hard he looked, and he had a teenage daughter and three young boys to support. The daughter, though she was still officially too young to work full-time, knew that these things were often overlooked. So she went to the mill her mother used to work in, the Coffin Mill, and she asked to see the overseer. He was a man, of course. And she told him the situation the family was in, how they were struggling to keep the roof over their heads and getting into debt just to feed themselves. Well, a woman's wage was still cheap labour, and the demand for jute was booming so they could always use more hands. That same day, she started work as a spinner.

She was so relieved to have a job, and to know that her wee brothers would be fed and clothed through the winter. But the bairns would need shoes soon, and they still owed the grocer some money, and if they could get her dad's coat back from the pawn shop before the cold weather started … She was a young woman with a lot of worries, and she was quiet and withdrawn among the chat and bustle of the mill. This was obvious to her workmates, who felt sorry for her – although many of them were in the same boat, she *was* awfy young to have the weight of a household on her shoulders, they thought. But it was obvious to the overseer as well, and he was not as sympathetic. He acted like it, though, always offering her overtime, which she never refused, and turning a blind eye if she was ever a couple of minutes late from getting her brothers ready for school in the morning. He even managed the odd smile for her when he came round to inspect the women's work.

One day, he came to find the girl at the end of the afternoon shift. He said he knew that she was having a hard time and he would see what he could do to support her family – if she came up to his office they could speak about it. As the rest of the workers poured out of the mill, they went to the deserted upper floor. Once they were in his office, the overseer locked the door behind them.

'I've been doing you a lot of favours lately,' he said, 'and it's time you paid me back for them. Don't look at me like that – you know what I'm talking about.' She didn't speak a word through the whole encounter.

After that day, as the months went on, the girl's workmates noticed she seemed even more troubled. She came in and stood silently at her machine for her shift, then left. And although she laced her stays more tightly, they'd seen a girl trying to hide a pregnancy before. It was obvious she was in trouble. And one morning, with the heat, and the work, and the discomfort of her tight corset, she fainted dead away in the middle of the mill floor. One of her neighbours quickly reached out and began to work her machine as well, so she wouldn't lose the day's pay, and the mill's cleaner, an old woman who'd seen a lot in her time, got her out of the way and found her a drink of water in a quiet corner. When she came to, the old woman asked her: 'Are you going to be all right? Whose is it, is he looking after you?'

The girl sighed.

'It's *his*,' she whispered, head tilting towards the overseer on his rounds. 'And I've no told him. Don't want to gie him the satisfaction.'

Well, there's no keeping a secret in a busy mill. By dinner time the whole place was abuzz with the rumour, and the overseer noticed that the women were giving him even blacker looks than normal as he did his rounds. As he passed the young girl's machine, he told her that she'd better stay behind after her shift that day. They had a matter to discuss.

She spent the afternoon under a black cloud. What if she lost her job? She wouldn't be able to hide her pregnancy much longer, so she wouldn't be hired anywhere else. Her brothers would still need food, and soon there'd be a baby … But maybe he was a better man than he seemed, maybe he was going to tell her he would give the bairn his name.

At six o'clock that day, a group of women lingered by the mill gates. They knew what was happening, and they wanted to be there for the young lass if she emerged in tears. The overseer had no idea he had witnesses as he pulled the girl out onto the narrow iron bridge which crossed the courtyard. They could see they were arguing, she was pleading with him – but then he struck her across the head, and pushed her dazed body over the railing. She hurtled towards the cobbles below. Although her workmates rushed back into the yard towards her, it was too late. She was dead.

Ever since then, her spirit returns to the bridge to relive her last moments. Known as the White Lady of the Coffin Mill, her pale figure can be seen wandering out into the middle of the bridge, then falling to her doom.

There are several versions of the story of how the White Lady of the Coffin Mill came to be, but they all agree that she haunts the bridge in particular. In 1945, when the Coffin Mill was being used as a furniture warehouse, a reported sighting of the White Lady caused chaos as people tried to break into the mill to see the ghost, and the police had to disperse an agitated crowd. The Coffin Mill has since been converted into flats, but the bridge – and presumably the White Lady – are still there.

There is another haunted bridge too, not very far from the Coffin Mill. At Balgay, a blue and red cast-iron bridge spans a gap between two hills – one home to a wooded public park and observatory, and the other a graveyard. A White Lady haunts this bridge too, appearing to people who cross it. She is said to be the ghost of a broken-hearted widow who died when she threw herself from the bridge.

COSSACK JOCK

In the days before the rail bridge was built over the Tay, the only way to cross the river to Fife was, of course, by ferry. One of the most famous ferrymen to steer this route was a man named John Spalding, known to all as Cossack Jock. He was a tall, imposing man with a long black beard, and he was well known as a skilled boatman and for the ballads he sang as he guided his ferry, the *Nelson*, between the city and the little town of Newport across the water.

The spring of 1815 was a terrible one for weather, with March storms howling on well into April and beyond. Many a crossing had to be abandoned that year. By the time late May wore on, it seemed the weather was settling down, and the sailors on the Tay began to relax. But one Sunday afternoon at the end of May, Cossack Jock was halfway across the river with his boat full of passengers when the sky suddenly darkened and the winds whipped up. There was one last storm to come, and it was a bad one. The *Nelson* was tossed from side to side on the waves. Jock did his best to keep her upright, but in the end she went down with all twenty-two passengers. The harbourmaster, looking powerless from the shore, said he saw Jock flailing about in the wreckage, trying to keep passengers afloat until the bitter end. But there was no saving any of them.

Jock's body was found last of all. He washed up at the Craig Pier, not far from his own little house. As the custom was then, he was laid out in his home before the funeral, surrounded by candles. All the seafaring community from Dundee – sailors, fishwives, fishermen and harbour-men – came by to pay their last respects. Cossack Jock made a very imposing corpse. His tall body seemed even larger in death. But the house buzzed with people recounting memories and singing the old ballads he was once known for.

All of a sudden, the talking and singing was interrupted by a gasp from a mourner by Jock's bedside. The folk looked over and saw, in the flickering candlelight, a movement around his arm. His hand seemed to be shifting from his side beneath the sheet. At once, everyone shrieked and rushed to the door, blocking the exit as they fought to escape the icy clutches of the revenant. Those who had not made it out watched as the movement continued up the side of Jock's body, his hand slowly making its way towards his head at the top of the sheet, fingers crawling their way up the bed ... Those that could still bear to watch the dreadful movement were pressed against the far wall in horror of what awaited them.

Crash! The loud clattering sound that followed shocked everyone. Looking to the bed, they saw, crawling its way out of the trailing sheet onto the floor, a huge black crab.

'It's the Devil!' shrieked one of the mourners. Now, people were happy to huddle around the corpse to give the satanic beast a wide berth as it scuttled sideways for the door. The cries of 'Satan!' and 'Evil!' had reached the streets outside, and a growing crowd stood – at a safe distance – to see what would emerge from the cottage. The crab, sensing the sea nearby, scuttled off towards the harbour at a gallop, people diving out of its way as if it was on fire. All the crab wanted was a clear run back to the safety of the sea, and the creature looked like it was in luck. Until across its path wandered old Creel Katie. Katie was an old wife who wandered the shores, beachcombing and gathering this and that. She made a swipe for the back legs of the crab, caught it, and dangled it in front of the horrified audience.

'What for would you lot let such a braw big partan go?'
she asked.

'Leave him, Katie!' they yelled back. 'He's no canny! It's no
crab, it's the Devil himself!'

But Devil or crab, Katie was not fazed. She promised him a
good long simmer in the pot that evening, for herself and her
gudeman Davie, who had not been keeping well, and that is
exactly what she did. Her neighbours said that they had seen a
gust of black smoke reeking of pitch and brimstone come from
her chimney as she cooked, and out of her door and windows
as well, and others said that they had seen Auld Clootie himself
come flying out of the chimney, complete with horns, hooves
and tail.

But Katie said that it was as sweet a bit of crab as she had ever
eaten, and what's more, it had helped her gudeman out of his
illness – not something she thought the Devil likely to do for
such a kind and Christian body as her Davie.

*The story of Cossack Jock was first made popular by the poet
Thomas Hood, who spent his summers with family in Dundee and
was in the city when the* Nelson *sank. The historian A.H. Millar,
writing just over a century later in 1923, heard from a woman in
Tayport whose mother had remembered the great stooshie over the
Devil Crab at Jock's wake.*

THE BANSHEE CAT OF BLACKNESS

Before the Second World War, the site which is now Blackness
Road Fire Station was known as Cherryfield. A man named
Harry Beattie owned a yard there, and when Traveller families
were in town this was one of the places they'd camp.

Once a family with a young daughter was staying there.
When the girl went out to play one day, she came across a little

black kitten wandering the streets of Blackness. It seemed like it was a stray, and the wee creature was adorable, gazing up at her with big amber eyes from a soft black face. She couldn't bear to leave the kitten to fend for itself.

Now, her father had a very strict rule about not keeping pets in the caravan. This was for good reason – there was little enough space for the family as it was, and an animal could cause any amount of chaos. But she thought if she could keep the kitten hidden for a few days, that would prove just how little trouble it was, and her dad might relent. So she hid the tiny cat below her jumper when she went in to her bed, and sneaked it below the covers in her bunk. The two of them curled up together, the kitten purring away as she drifted off to sleep.

But the kitten did not sleep. Under cover of dark, it padded down from the bed and crept around the shadows of the caravan as the family snored.

The girl's father was the first to wake up. He heard a dull thud and thought one of his bairns must be up making mischief. But when he looked towards the sound he saw a terrible sight. The kitten was no longer tiny – it was a black panther-like beast, about the size of a Rottweiler but angrier, with horns on either side of its head and glowing eyes that shone so bright they cast light around the whole caravan. It breathed a smoky, sulphurous breath that made him choke. And as he looked at it, the thing was growing bigger.

He cried out and told his family to get up, quick, and run outside. Then he tried to wrestle this demon cat out of his home, knocking cups on the floor and trailing bedsheets as they fought. Eventually, he dragged the creature out of the door and the family all watched it tear off towards Balgay, howling and screeching in the night.

When they decided it was safe to go back inside, among the chaos they saw the family Bible was lying on the floor, its pages splayed open. The father picked it up. He shivered as he saw the cat's pawprint burnt into the page. Then he read the words upon which the mark was centred. It was the Book of Revelations, and the verse read: *And the first beast was like a lion.*

The creature, they thought, must have been so angered by coming across the word of God in the caravan that it had shown its true demonic form. For years afterwards people spoke in horror of the banshee cat of Blackness. And I don't think the girl ever tried to sneak a pet home again either.

J. Burke, who included this in their Dundee ghost story collection Dinnae Fleg The Bairns, *heard the story from the girl herself after she had grown up.*

6

JACOBITE ESCAPES

Most of the big families in Angus supported the Jacobite cause, and plenty of their tenants and workers joined them in the Rebellions of 1715 and 1745. After defeat at Culloden in 1746, the Angus Regiment of Jacobites marched back to Glen Clova, and from there, knowing there was a price on their heads, they all made their separate ways into hiding or into exile.

BONNYMUNE'S CAVE

The rebel laird Balnamoon took to the hills after Culloden, hiding out near his home in Glenmark. His new residence was a cave near the foot of Curmaud Hill, which ran deep but had only a small opening to the world and was hard to spot. It was a cold and dark home, though luckily Balnamoon had many friends in the area who would bring him supplies and invite him into their houses to get warm.

The suspicious minister of the parish noticed these odd comings and goings, and he began to figure out that the folk of Glenmark were up to something. This minister had no sympathy for the Episcopalians at all and would be glad to see the back of them in his parish. So he spread the word of Balnamoon's whereabouts.

A group of soldiers arrived on a cold and wet winter's night. They stormed into the kitchen of a farmhouse where Balnamoon himself was sitting, warming himself by the fire. But in the rough clothes he wore in his exile, the laird could pass for a farm servant.

'Away ye go,' the farmer said roughly. 'Mak yersel useful and clean oot the byre, and gie oor guests a seat at the fire.'

Balnamoon did not need telling twice. He walked out past the soldiers, and as soon as he was out of the farmhouse, ran like a deer until he was safely concealed in his cave.

That place has become known as Bonnymune's Cave, in honour of its most celebrated (and probably only) inhabitant. The laird, like many of his fellow wealthy Jacobites, got his land and his title back in the fullness of time, and when that happened, he saw that the farmer who helped him out was richly rewarded.

The Men of Lintrathen

The men of Lintrathen were almost all out for Charlie in the '45 rebellion. All except for a man named John Peter, whose home was at Pitmudie at the north end of the Loch of Lintrathen. This meant John Peter was left in charge of all the farms in the district. John was not in favour of Bonnie Prince Charlie, but he was in favour of Lintrathen, so he did his best to keep things running and he did not betray his neighbours after the rebellion failed.

In the months after Culloden, the Angus glens were full of soldiers seeking out the rebels they knew were hiding somewhere, and there were plenty hidden around the hills at Lintrathen. The soldiers came with strict orders to burn the buildings and seize the cattle of any rebel farmers. They would investigate every herd of cattle and demand to know who they belonged to. And everywhere they stopped between Kilry and Kingoldrum, there was John Peter, popping up again and calling to them, 'Aye, they're my kye, leave them be!' They suspected, but there was nothing they could do to prove otherwise.

On another visit, the soldiers came across a young lad, far too young to have been at Culloden himself.

'Where have you been today, son?' they asked him.

He'd just returned from dropping off food for the rebels hiding up the glen, but he knew better than to admit it.

'Just away seeing to my faither's kye,' he replied.

'So what's your bag there for, then? You're not taking food out to the rebels, are you?'

'Naw, it's just for my denner,' said the boy. Then he noticed one of the soldiers wore a drum slung across his chest. The boy's eyes widened in wonder. 'Fat a braw wee tub that is! Dae ye keep your pieces in that?'

The soldiers roared with laughter. These country fools up here have never seen a drum!

'Go on, give him a roll on it,' their leader laughed. So the drummer struck up a *rat-a-tat-tat* and the young lad leapt backwards in shock at the sound of it. As he got to his feet and started to step back towards the soldiers, the drummer gave another thundering roll and the boy cried out in fright again. The soldiers were doubled over with laughing.

Meanwhile, up in the hills, the hidden Jacobites heard the drum and knew it was time to make themselves scarce. The boy was nowhere near as daft as he looked.

When one of the old Lintrathen rebels was captured and taken before the commissioners at Forfar, he decided his best plan was to pretend to be deaf. Everything the commissioners said was met with a blank stony expression. But they suspected he was at it, so they got a band to come in and play some music. Surely his face would show something as they played the most emotive songs they could think of. Still nothing. Then the colonel who had brought him in suggested they tried 'The Auld Stuart is Back Again'. If he could hear anything, he'd hear that – and as the strains of the Jacobite anthem filled the Forfar courthouse, sure enough he could not help but nod his head in time to its music.

'Since you can hear us now, how about you ask for the king's pardon and we'll let you go?' said the colonel. But the stubborn man refused.

'Hang him!' cried the commissioners. But the colonel had come to respect his obstinacy.

'If his life's no worth the asking, it's hardly worth the taking of it,' said the colonel, and sent him packing.

LORD OGILVY'S PORRIDGE

Lord Ogilvy led the Angus Regiment of Jacobites at Culloden. Afterwards, he and his faithful servant John Thomson were on the run together. The two of them swapped clothes, in the hope this would make them harder to recognise. They made their way along the foothills of the Grampians, being sure to avoid Cortachy, where everyone suspected Ogilvy might make his way home to. One night they took lodgings at a tiny inn. This was a rough and ready sort of establishment, the kind of place where travellers made their own meals at the kitchen fire.

As the 'servant' of the pair, it stood to reason that Ogilvy would be the one to cook their supper. But being a lord in disguise, this was not a thing at which he'd had much practice. John looked on in horror as Lord Ogilvy chucked handfuls of oatmeal into the pot. The thought of having to eat the lumpy paste Ogilvy was cooking up after days of starvation was too much, and before he could stop himself, John begged him, 'Twinkle your little finger, my lord, twinkle your little finger!'

As soon as the words were out, he realised his mistake. There was no knowing who might have overheard. So the two of them had to abandon the inn, porridge and all. It was another night on the hills for them.

7

Wells and Saints

Legend has it there have been a few saints among the folk of Angus. Many have visited too, as the Picts took a lot of converting to bring them into Christianity. It was said that three saints visited the area around Tannadice and Cortachy – St Ninian, his follower St Ternance, and St Arnold. They are remembered in local place names, like Saint Arnold's Seat near Glen Ogil. Often, saints are connected with wells or springs, and at one time folk would have been able to point you to a healing spring in every parish.

St Donivald and the Nine Maidens

In the eighth century, a Christian man named Donivald came to live among the Picts in Glen Ogilvy, along with his wife and nine young daughters. Donivald's wife died soon after they arrived, and the family turned to a simple and sparse life. They ate barley-bread and drank cold water, and that only once a day. But their faith was strong, and the girls walked for miles to help their father spread the word of God, tend to the sick and comfort the troubled.

But it was a hard living for them, especially in the colder months. Flocks of wild geese would fly over the glens and stop to eat all the grain from their small patch of barley. One day, the eldest daughter, whose name was Mazota, went out to the geese and said to them, 'Please leave us some barley. This is all we have, and we are hungry, too.' After that day, the family were never troubled by the geese again. That was the first sign that there was something special about the family.

Donivald and his daughters were well-loved by the folk round about. When Donivald died, the King of the Picts made sure that the nine young women were well looked after. He gave them a home and chapel at Abernethy in Fife, from where they continued their good works. When finally they grew old and died, they were buried there beneath a huge oak tree.

The Nine Maidens, as the women became known, were well remembered by the folk of Angus. A well at Glamis, a church at Finavon, and many other holy places, were dedicated to their memory. Their feast day is 15 June, and on that day, the young girls from Glamis used to walk to Abernethy in pilgrimage in their memory.

Among the places connected with the Nine Maidens may be Ninewells in Dundee, possibly a shortened form of 'Nine Maidens Well', which seems like an appropriately healing origin for a name now best known as the city's hospital. There is also a link between the nine maidens in this story and the nine daughters in the tale of the Strathmartine Dragon.

St Triduana

Another early Christian who came to Angus was a young Greek woman, whose name was Triduana. She came with Saint Rule when he brought the relics of Saint Andrew to the Pictish kings of Scotland, to the place in Fife which still bears the name of Scotland's patron saint. Triduana liked Scotland, and she decided to remain. She crossed the Tay and continued her journey north. When she came to Rescobie, near Forfar, she settled by the banks of the loch there among a small community. There, she found the life she had always wanted. She prayed and studied holy texts, and tended to the sick.

King Nechtan of the Picts lived not far from Rescobie. He was a powerful man and famed for miles. When he came by Rescobie and met Triduana, Nechtan immediately fell in love with her beauty. He asked for her hand in marriage, promising her all the wealth and influence she could ever dream of. But Triduana refused. Her life was here, and it was devoted to God. No man could change that. She sent him away.

Nechtan left that time, but he soon returned, and he did so again and again.

'Please,' he begged her. 'I love you so much. Please come and be my wife.'

One day, she came out from her cell at Rescobie to where Nechtan was standing outside it. She asked him, 'What is it that you love about me?'

Nechtan thought this was his chance. 'Your beautiful eyes,' he said. 'They shine like the sea and I cannot forget them.'

'Very well,' Triduana said. 'If it is my eyes that you love then you shall have them.' She broke a twig from the branch of a tree, and drove it into first one eye, gouging it out with the stick, and then the other. She held out the stick to Nechtan. 'They are yours.'

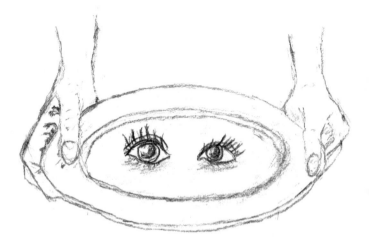

After that, Triduana had peace. She also had a divine gift. She was given the power to heal blindness and diseases of the eyes, and folk came from far and wide to be cured by her. For the rest of her life, Triduana travelled around Scotland, sharing her healing powers. When she came by Restalrig, at Arthur's Seat in Edinburgh, she stopped to wash at a spring there, and when she bathed her face, she found her own sight came back to her. Springs and lochs dedicated to Triduana can be found across Scotland, as far north as Papa Westray in Orkney, and their water is still sought by people suffering from afflictions of the eyes. St Troddan's Well near her former home in Rescobie was one of these, but its location is now lost.

Perhaps what Triduana did changed something in King Nechtan, too. By the end of his life, he too chose the path of solitude and quiet reflection. He was baptised as a Christian by Saint Boniface, and he ended his days in a monastery.

St Drostan's Well

Near Edzell, there was a well dedicated to Saint Drostan, and it was renowned for its healing powers. All the people from near and far relied on its power to heal any illnesses that came upon them. The well was, in fact, so powerful that it cured everything, and the two doctors in Edzell and Brechin could get no work.

Frustrated by this, the doctors resolved to poison the water of St Drostan's Well one night. But one of their servants overheard, and she whispered the news of what they were planning to the community. As the two doctors approached the well, they were set upon by a furious crowd of their neighbours, armed with sticks and forks. The doctors were beaten so thoroughly that they were beyond even the healing powers of the well. They were buried nearby, and no one dared to meddle with the waters of St Drostan's again.

The Healing Well of Benvie

The people in the small village of Benvie were once terrified by a ghost who walked the banks of the Invergowrie Burn by night. She was a mournful spirit, dressed in a long white robe. One night, the young minister got up the courage to go and speak to her, dressed in his full canonical robe with his Bible in his hand, and asked her who she was and why she haunted the place.

'Holy man,' she said, 'I was a victim of the Great Plague, and though I died here I was not from this parish, and so no one knew me. They buried me outside of the kirkyard. If you find my body and rebury me in consecrated ground, I will be at rest. And from the spot where my body lay, a spring of water will rise up, and this water will be a cure for any plagues to come.'

The minister promised he would do as she asked, and the ghost led him along the burn, where she pointed to a spot. In the morning, he returned with a spade and dug there. Sure enough, he soon came across a pale skeleton, wrapped in the same white shroud the ghost had worn. He carried the bones to Benvie Kirkyard and said a prayer as he buried her in her new resting place. As soon as the earth was closed over the new grave, a spring leapt up from the spot where she had lain. The ghost was never seen again, and for centuries the people of Benvie went to that spring for healing water.

8

Stones and Souterrains

The land of Angus bears the marks of previous residents, who left little or nothing in the way of written history but have passed down to us a wealth of carved stones, burial mounds, and the dark tunnels of the souterrains. Also known as 'earth houses', souterrains are one of the more distinctive archaeological features in the county. Tradition has it that these were Picts', or even fairies', houses (like in the story of the Laird of Balmachie), but they were probably used for storage or to shelter cattle. Over the years, supernatural stories have become anchored to the stones and mounds of Angus, warning us to be careful of the unseen forces we share this world with.

The Devil's Hand

One day, many years ago, the Devil was out taking his Sunday walk on the Fife side of the Tay estuary by Wormit Bay, when across the water he spied St Boniface building his church at Invergowrie. He was horrified to see this church-building lark had spread north of the Tay, and he decided to put a stop to it. So he picked up the biggest boulder he could see and hurled it across the river, hoping to hit the saint. But in his anger he overshot his mark, and the stone landed nearly a mile north of the church. It was too big for anyone to move it from its landing place, so there it stayed, where it lies to this very day, known as the Devil's Stone.

The Devil was not ready to give up after his missed shot. He picked up another two boulders and flung them towards the church, but this time he had not thrown them far enough. They landed in the water at the other side of the river, and sent such a splash of cold Tay water back over the Devil's legs that he gave up and humphed back to Hell to warm up. These two stones, which lay in the river at high water and out of it at low water, became known as the Goors o Gowrie. Folk said they carried a bit of devilry with them still, and each year they would inch a little bit closer to the church, with their original purpose still in mind. The seer Thomas the Rhymer had a prophecy about them, saying: 'When the Goors o Gowrie come to land, the Day of Judgement's near at hand.' Folk from Invergowrie and Dundee would go and examine the stones every year or so, to keep an eye on their journey.

No one is very sure which stones these are now, if they still exist. But in the nineteenth century, a lot of land was claimed from the Tay, and when the railway between Dundee and Perth was built, the tracks ran – as they still do – very close to the river. Some folk say the railway embankment was built between the Goors o Gowrie and the water. So that might have been them come to land at last, and if it was, it means we cannot be too far away from the Day of Judgement now. The Devil's Stone is also sometimes known as the Paddock Stane. It fell within the land on which wealthy industrialist David Watson built his home, Greystane House, in the 1860s. The house still stands and is currently in use as a hotel – the Devil's Stone can still be seen in its grounds.

On another occasion, the Devil took a holiday in the Angus glens, and he would have had a lovely time had it not been for having to listen to the minister at Cortachy Church slander him week on week. One Sunday he lost his temper and, using his old tactics, he looked around for a huge boulder to hurl at the church. But again his shot was off, by a whole fifteen miles! The boulder landed slap bang in the middle of the River Isla, where it too still remains. Although the water where the boulder fell is deep, it always stands above the water level. If you happen to see the boulder submerged, it is not a happy sight, for it means a death will soon come to the parish. The direction in which the water flows around the stone also indicates whether the next child born to the Airlie family will be a boy or a girl.

The River Isla has another way of foretelling bad news. The Reekie Linn waterfall, by Craigisla, is a beautiful and impressive sight, and you should definitely visit if you are in the area. But listen carefully if you do. Above the rush of foaming water, sometimes folk have heard shrieks and howls of pain and despair. And every time this has been heard, news of a death has soon followed – sometimes the listener's own death.

WITCHES AND FAIRY FOLK

Witches and fairies have left their mark on the landscape too. Near the foot of Glen Lethnot, the hills of the Brown and White Caterthuns look out over Strathmore. These hills were to be home to a great and powerful witch, who planned to build a tower on each so that she could look down over Angus. She went down to the West Water and began gathering stones in her apron so that she could carry them up to begin building. With a morning's work, she made a good start on her towers, and the foundations are still there on the tops of the Caterthuns. But when she was making her way up the north side of the White Caterthun with a particularly big stone, her apron string snapped and the stone fell to the ground. In disgust, she gave up, and the stone still lies where it fell.

The Girdle Stane of Dunnichen was another one dropped by a witch, who had been carrying it north from the Crafts of Carmyllie when her apron string broke. No doubt this witch had been visiting supernatural kin in Carmyllie, for Carmyllie Hill was once well known as an abode of the fairies. Near the top of the hill there was a tumulus known as Fairyfolk Hillock, where the fairy folk could be seen dancing and revelling in the night. Despite this, when Carmyllie was to get its church, the hill was settled on as the best spot for the building – higher, the thinking went, was closer to God.

But though the builders worked all day, they always arrived in the morning to find the stones they had laid the day before scattered around and torn down. Determined to catch the culprits, the builders vowed to stay at the site all night and catch whoever was creeping in. They set up watch in a circle around the hill, so no one could approach without being spotted. No one arrived all night, and they thought they must have deterred the destroyer at last. But when the men returned to the top of the hill at dawn, they found the foundations in ruins yet again – although they each swore they had seen nobody. And then they heard a voice, coming seemingly from nowhere – or from the earth itself:

> Build not on this enchanted spot
> Where man has neither part nor lot
> But build thee doon in yonder bog
> Where it will neither shake nor shog.

When they heard these words, they knew there was no point in arguing, and so Carmyllie Parish Church was built on low ground to the south of the hill, where it still stands.

The tumulus known as Fairyfolk Hillock was a prehistoric grave mound – stone coffins were found there during an excavation in the 1830s. A similar story of fairies interrupting building, along with a similar rhyme, was also told about Glamis Castle, with nearby Hunter's Hill being the planned site. In recent years, Carmyllie

has seen reported sightings of a Bigfoot-like creature lurking in the
woods. Perhaps it remains a place where the other world makes its
presence felt more than usual.

GREENFIELD KNOWE

The farmer of Greenfield at Auchterhouse was improving his land. He had plans to build dykes around some of the fields. While he was at it, he planned to get rid of the two boulders which lay on Greenfield Knowe and make more space for his crops. One morning, he asked his workers to shift these boulders and make them part of the dyke. One by one, all his men shook their heads, looking darkly at the ground. There was no way they were touching these stones. These were witches' stones, they said. To move them would bring bad fortune to them and their families.

The farmer sighed. He did not believe a word of this, but he could not persuade them to do it for anything, and they were too big to move by himself. He decided to give it a night's sleep and make a decision on how to handle them the following day.

But as he lay in bed that night, he kept turning the issue over and over in his mind. Should he bribe the men, or threaten them? And in the midst of that wakeful night, the farmer saw a pale figure come striding into his bedroom. It came up right to the side of his bed and fixed him in its shadowy gaze. And in a deep, grave voice he heard: 'Gang ower the howe tae anither knowe.'

Then the thing faded into the darkness.

The farmer slept not a wink that night. First thing next morning, he told his workers not to worry. The stones would stay exactly where they were.

Another generation or so down the line, there was an old man of Auchterhouse who was undertaking some repairs to his crumbling old cottage. Being a make-do and mend sort of person, he attempted to incorporate some old stones into the walls rather than paying for newly quarried ones – including the stones from Greenfield Knowe. He carted them off and built them into his walls. Well, as you might imagine by now, the first night in his newly renovated house was not a peaceful one. He was kept awake by a cold, haunting feeling of dread and the most intense guilt – so intense, in fact, that he could bear it no longer. He arose in the middle of the night, undid his day's work to remove the stones, and carted the two Greenfield stones back to their rightful place in the dark, rather than have to lie with the feeling until dawn.

But it seems that eventually someone who could stand living with a haunted conscience developed the land at Auchterhouse, because the two cup-and-ring stones recorded on old maps, which were known locally as 'The Witch's Stones', are no longer there.

St Orland's Stone

St Orland's Stone, an elaborately carved Pictish slab, stands almost at the mid-point of a triangle with Kirrie to the north, Forfar to the east, and Glamis to the south-west. St Orland's Stone is said to be a wise stone. If your mind is troubled by some question, make your way to the stone – at midnight, if you can – and ask for guidance. St Orland's Stone might speak, or give some physical sign, or help you find the answer inside yourself, but somehow it will bring you your answer.

The stone is particularly wise in settling matters of the heart, and it was for this reason that young Helen Lindsay, a crofter's daughter from Cossans, decided to consult it. You see, Helen had quite a dilemma on her hands. She had two suitors who had declared their love for her – a young carpenter from her village, and the son of the farmer at Drumgley over by Forfar.

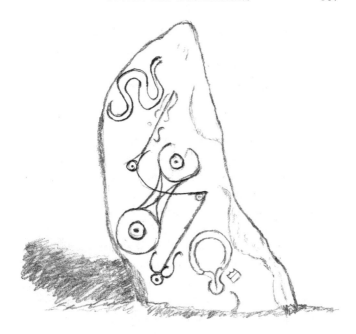

And Helen did not find it an easy choice. Both young men were good company, good looking, and had good prospects, and she genuinely was equally fond of them both.

Helen was an honest lass, and she wanted to be fair to the boys too.

'Lads,' she said, 'I really like both of you, and I just don't know how to choose between you. And since I like you both, I'd hate to hurt either one of you.'

The young men were both level-headed fellows and they saw no use in fighting or falling out over it either. The three of them decided that they would let St Orland's Stone make the choice. One night at midnight, Helen and her two lads would all meet at the stone, and they would take whatever answer it gave them. There was only one condition to this arrangement – if any one of the three failed to turn up at the appointed hour, that would be taken to mean that they had withdrawn their interest.

The morning after they had all shaken hands on this, the carpenter heard some sad news. An old friend of his was dead, and the funeral was to be on the same day that they had arranged to visit the stone. But he saw no reason that he could not go to the funeral in the forenoon and be back long before midnight.

The funeral procession was to begin at Murroes, at the farm where the man had died, and make its way to Glamis, where he was to be laid to rest with his family. There was no hearse in the parish of Murroes in those days, so the coffin was laid in a farm cart and covered with the parish mortcloth. It was in this humble fashion that the procession of mourners made their way uphill towards the Forfar road. Only the small group of pall-bearers, of whom the carpenter was one, were expected to make the long trek by foot. In these days, it was not the custom for women to go to the graveside, so they turned back to Murroes after a little while and left the men to walk on.

It was hard work walking alongside the cart, and it was a hot day, and when they got to Tealing the men decided that they should stop to refresh themselves and toast their friend. It was what he would have wanted. So they parked the cart, the horse and the coffin in a little layby at the roadside, and they made their way to the roadside inn.

The first pint went down very well, so they thought they'd better have another, and then perhaps a wee dram since it was traditional, but that needed another beer to go with it … and then the sun was looking very low in the sky indeed. From the drunken haze he was sinking into, the carpenter remembered his tryst that night, and leapt to his feet.

'It's time we got him to Glamis afore it's dark!' he cried. The others looked up from their drams and realised he had a point – lugging coffins about in the dark was no one's idea of fun. So, a little more shakily than before, they headed out to resume the procession.

But when they got to the roadside, there was no cart to be seen. And there was no horse either. And there was certainly no coffin.

The men searched down every lane, round the back of every building, and in every byre in Tealing. There was no sign of cart, or horse, or coffin.

'It's the Deil that's taen him,' said one. 'I tellt you he was up to something afore he died.'

'Could the Deil no have taen him at Murroes and saved us a walk? Besides, surely he'd have his own transport and no need to tak oors.'

But there was no other possible explanation, or at least not one that they could come up with in the state they were in.

'Och weel,' said somebody. 'We'd best gang back doon the road and see what we can dae the morn.'

Now the carpenter had his own dilemma. He could make his way back through the gloaming on his own and get back to Glamis in time to meet the other two at St Orland's Stone. But what was he to say to the grieving family when he turned up, the sole survivor of the funeral procession, with no idea where the corpse was? No, that did not bear thinking about. So, glumly, he trudged back down the road to Murroes with the others, back to the farm where they had started their journey.

And there stood the horse, patiently waiting in the yard with the cart and coffin still firmly attached. The poor creature had waited on them for a few hours outside the inn, and eventually decided it had been deserted for good. Then it had made its way home along the familiar road.

They had some explaining to do to the women of the funeral party, who had been sharing their own memories of the departed over tea – and maybe the occasional brandy – in the farmhouse. But at least there was a cheerful occasion to look forward to not so long after – the wedding of Helen Lindsay to the young farmer at Drumgley.

THE ADDER STONE

In the Burn of Calletar there once stood a pale grey stone, famous in the local area for having a hole in its centre large enough to reach your arm through. This was known as the Adder Stone, for the reason that white adders were somehow compelled towards the stone. On a sunny day, you could stand and watch the white adders chase each other in and out of the stone, whirling through and through the hole. Adder stones were valuable to those with knowledge of such things, for there was great power to be gained from them. The stone itself was a protection – animals, or indeed people, whose sickness was suspected to have a supernatural origin would be brought to the stone in search of healing. As for the adders, they held their own magic. It was said that whatever effort you made to catch an adder, the power you gained from it would repay that effort tenfold.

There was, in the early nineteenth century, a wise man in the parish of Lethnot who caught one of the adders drawn to the stone, and boiled it up to make a broth. Drinking the white adder's broth bestows the second sight upon a person, and so it was for this man. He was always in great demand for his cures and knowledge. One day, a farmer whose cattle were struck by a mysterious illness sent for the wise man to come and help. The wise man filled a bowl of water from the burn, and from his pocket he took a small ball of polished steel. Holding the ball over the water, and murmuring some long-forgotten incantations, the farmer was astonished to see in the bowl appeared the face of an old woman, one of his own cottars. This was the culprit who was putting the sickness onto the cattle.

The name of this witch, if a witch she was, has not been recorded. But when the historian Andrew Jervise was compiling his *History and Traditions of the Land of the Lindsays*, she was still well-remembered in the parish. One lifelong Lethnot resident told Jervise that he made the mistake of referring to her as a witch within sight of her cottage, while he was driving one of his father's carts as a youth. Some unseen hand cowped over his cart of lime three times that day.

Another spot said to be home to white adders was behind Reekie Linn near Craigisla.

The Airlie Souterrain

Around 1800, a cottar woman who lived at Barns of Airlie had a problem with her hearth. Instead of having to clean out the ashes of her fire each morning, hers vanished into thin air. Her neighbours said that this was not a problem at all and they would be glad to swap hearths with her, but something about it felt uncanny. One day, she had a good fire going and was baking oatcakes, in the old-fashioned way, toasting them on a bannock stone in the hearth. She saw one began to slip off the stone and leant forwards to shift it back into place. But in front of her eyes it slid clean off the stone – and vanished.

That was as much as her nerves could take and she ran to her neighbours, begging them to let her stay for a while. They were intrigued, and they decided there must be something in the house itself which had made these strange things happen. The neighbours offered to take down the whole structure and rebuild it, to see if that would settle her mind. So out came her few plates and cups and chairs, and off came the thatch on the roof, and soon the walls were down as well. There was nothing odd to be seen so far. Her cottage was earth-floored and so there were no floorboards to pull up, just the flagstones of the hearth. The neighbours eased them up using a length of wood as a lever. As the stones came away from the ground, they revealed something nobody had expected. Below the hearth, there emerged a long dark tunnel, curving down into the earth. It was clearly made by human hands – the sides were fully lined with huge stones, and there were flat stone slabs running across the roof. This must have been the mouth that had been swallowing ashes and bannocks. After all, there's no such thing as fairies, is there?

9

Hidden Treasures

Here are four stories of riches lying below the ground of Angus. The earth – or the power which guards it – is reluctant to surrender its wealth to human hands.

The Hill of Kirriemuir

On the Hill of Kirriemuir stands a stone, the only survivor of a stone circle. One side of the stone looks south to the Sidlaw Hills, and the other looks north to the Grampians. The surviving stone used to be twice the height it is today, and this is the story of how it broke.

On a busy market day in Kirrie, three outlaws teamed up to rob a man. Two of them caused a scene and distracted him, while one stole the heavy purse of gold from his pocket. The three of them quickly disappeared into the crowd and made for the hill before they could be caught. They hid behind the standing stone, on the Sidlaw side, to divide their spoils. Their plan was to scatter off in separate directions. As they counted the coins, there was a great creaking overhead. The men looked up just in time to see their fate coming towards them, as half the stone split away and crashed down onto their heads. They were crushed flat into the ground, and there they still lie, along with all their gold. Although generations of Kirrie folk have known that good treasure is buried there, none have dared to try to lift the stone and take it, for legend has it the same fate will befall anyone else who tries to touch the ill-gotten gold.

CASTLE VAYNE

On the banks of the Noran Water are the ruins of Castle Vayne, and below them, deep in the castle's old dungeon, lies a pile of gold and jewels which no one has laid eyes on for centuries. Many years ago, the inhabitants of the castle had to leave in a hurry when invaders threatened them. They tossed their fortune into the dungeon, hoping that it would not be found and that they could return to claim it later. But none of them lived long enough.

Many people have gone in search of this treasure over the years, but only one ever came close. One man, after searching the ruins, found the passageway leading down to the dungeon. He began to make his way down, imagining how the riches would change his life. Eventually, he came to a door in a stone wall. When he put his hand forward to try the door, out of the darkness roared a great horned ox. It roared with a burning hot breath that knocked him head over heels halfway back up the passage. Then the uncanny beast roared once more and disappeared through the solid wall with a blaze of flames lighting up around it.

He ran for his life out of the passage, and no amount of promised treasure would get him to set foot in it again. The doorway to the dungeon of Vayne has never been sighted since.

MELGUND CASTLE

There is another mysterious passageway at Melgund Castle, near Aberlemno. The last laird to live at Melgund was a man who liked to have the best of everything, and he spent well beyond even his sizeable means. He turned to gambling to improve his situation, but he had no luck at it, and soon he owed every coin, jewel and candlestick in the castle to one creditor or another. But he could not face up to a life of poverty. One night, when he knew the debt collectors were coming, he took his wife and children and all the valuable things he could carry deep into a tunnel below the castle, and he locked himself and his family away there. Now, whether he lost the key in the darkness or whether he was too afraid to come out ever again, nobody knows, but that was the last that was ever seen of them. The passage has lain sealed off for centuries.

Once, a brave young man thought he would have a go at getting into the passageway. He thought there must be a good hoard of wealth down there, and after all, there are worse things than skeletons. Like poverty, for instance. So, lantern in hand, he made his way down into the bowels of the earth, with a band of friends gathered at the entrance eagerly awaiting his return.

He was gone a long time. No sound came from the passage, and there was no sign of his lantern when his friends peered into the dark after him. As the day wore on they began to get very worried. Then the young man reappeared. He was white-faced and shaking, and empty-handed.

'What's down there?' they asked him. 'What did you see?'

'The tunnel goes a great way down,' he said, 'and I have seen such sights as I pray God I will never see on earth again!'

And that was all he could be persuaded to tell about his adventure.

Kettles of Silver and Gold

The fairies have their silver and gold too. Many years ago they hid a kettle of silver at the Craig of Stonyford, by Wirran. It is well hidden, but when the sun shines full on it, it can be seen glinting and sparkling in the sunlight. They hid a kettle of gold too, down in a well on the Hill of the Brown Caterthun. Although you might be tempted to search for either of these treasures, it would be a bad idea. It is said that whoever tries to take either of these treasures from their hiding place will be struck down by instant death. What's more, their afterlife will be one of constant labour until the end of the world. And once the world ends, they will be transported to an eternity of endless lamenting. So if you see a silvery glint while out hillwalking and are drawn in by the promise of riches – be wary.

Some of Angus's hidden treasures have allowed themselves to be found. The King of the Picts lost his crown on the banks of the Elliot Water, while travelling past Arbirlot. It lay where it fell for centuries, but was eventually found by a local farm labourer in 1700. Curious to find out more about its age and value, he sent it to an expert in London who promised to return it with more information, but he never did. The crown was lost once again.

In Glenesk, there is a pool in the North Esk known as Gracie's Linn, after a poor soul named Gracie who once drowned there. But that part of the river was also said to be a place of plenty. Sometimes, the river bed would be covered in gold, so much so that passers-by could go home with full pockets and a new fortune.

10

Weel-Kent Faces and Wee Stories

Anecdotes and stories of local worthies can be the most enduring in a place's folklore. Here are just a few of the hundreds of wee stories which have been told around Angus and Dundee.

John Gudefellow

John Gudefellow was a well-known figure in the glens. His home was at Navar. Since he had been born without legs, he travelled by swinging himself along on his hands, and asked for the food and clothing that he needed from the folk of the glens. But John had a fair temper on him, and he could be very demanding. One day he arrived at a farmhouse and asked for one thing after another. Finally, he demanded a meal of fried collops. The farmer's wife had no collops and no patience left either. She looked out a pair of old leather breeches, cut them into little pieces and fried them up with some onions and butter. John ate the whole thing delightedly, and remarked: 'Aye, lass – your collops are teuch but tasty.'

Hairy Kail

There were more strange characters in Victorian Dundee than we will ever have time to explore, but one of the most memorable was a man who had the nickname Hairy Kail. And the story of how he got it is not a pleasant one.

'Hairy' lived with his mother, and, like many folk did, she would put on a big pot of soup in the morning. The soup had a lot of other things in it besides kail, but everyone just referred to it as kail. One day, once the soup was bubbling away, his mother went away out to run some errands. Now, today's soup was special as there was a good chunk of mutton in it, which was not something they could afford every day. And it was tempting the lad. He kept going over to the pot and lifting the lid and inhaling the smell of it. Then he thought, surely if he tasted just a wee bit, his mother would never miss it. So he fished out a wee bit of the mutton and tasted it, and it was delicious. And he took a wee bit more, and a wee bit more, and a wee bit more until all the meat was gone.

When he realised he'd eaten all the mutton out of the kail, he was horrified. His mother would kill him! He'd better replace it with something. But what?

He grabbed the family cat and thrust it into the pot, shoving the lid down on the yowling, thrashing mess. And when his mother got home, he was so pleased by his solution that he called out, 'Hairy kail the day mither, hairy kail the day!'

I have also heard a modern version of this Dundee urban legend which involves an unfortunate cat falling into the deep fat fryer in a chip shop, and people being served up hairy chips.

THE SLUG CURE

In a cottage in Bonnethill – as the Hilltown of Dundee was once known, since this was where the bonnet-weavers had their homes – there lived two bonny sisters. The plague came to ravage Dundee, and people were sick and dying everywhere. It led to a famine for the folk of the Bonnethill too, because nobody was buying cloth, so they had no work. But throughout this horrible year, these two young women seemed to stay hale and healthy. No one could figure out how they managed it.

It was only when they were accused of witchcraft that the sisters shared how they had survived with no assistance. For a year they had eaten the black slugs which crawled up the damp walls of the Bonnethill cottages, and it turned out these were a guarantee of good health even against plague and famine.

THE AUCHTERHOUSE SMUGGLERS

In the days of whisky smuggling, Auchterhouse was the Sidlaws' answer to a wild frontier town. Dundee had a thirst for whisky, and the folk of the glens had illicit stills. And on the journey between them, all roads led to Auchterhouse. Its inhabitants were only too happy to get involved in the smuggling process in exchange for some money or a share of the cargo. They devised plenty of clever ways to get the drink into Dundee – some women would hide a pig's bladder filled with whisky under their skirts, others would install a false wooden

bottom in their milk pails and hide a layer of whisky below. But the whisky coming down from the glens came in big ten-gallon barrels, which the people of Auchterhouse would hide around hedges and farms.

Of course, the government knew people were trying to get around the rules, so they hired excisemen, known as gaugers, to go around inspecting likely places for evidence and apprehending anyone they suspected of smuggling. In 1813, a band of gaugers came across ninety-five gallons of whisky hidden among the corn in a field by Auchterhouse. They loaded it up onto their cart and set off to take the barrels back to Dundee, where I'm sure the officials would have made sure it was responsibly destroyed. But as they made their way south through Auchterhouse, they realised the distillers were not ready to give up so easily. Three Highlanders leapt out from the undergrowth, hurling stones and thrashing the gaugers with sticks. They battled for an hour or more, and the gaugers just about managed to hold their attackers off. Then a couple of Auchterhouse farmers passed by on the road. The gaugers were relieved – help was sure to come from these law-abiding citizens. But the farmers nodded to the Highlanders and carried on their way down the road.

That wasn't enough to put the excisemen off returning to Auchterhouse for more raids. On another occasion, they paid a visit to the biggest farm in the area. When the farmer saw them coming up the road, his heart must have sunk, for scattered around his byres and outhouses were several barrels of the finest Highland whisky. But he had an idea, and quickly set his men to work.

When the gaugers arrived, the farmer welcomed them in and offered them a large dram each before they went about their inspection. Never dreaming that anyone would dare to offer excisemen a contraband dram, they accepted, and as they drank, the farmer leaned against the kitchen table – just happening to block the view from the window of his men hurrying away into the fields with containers of whisky. When the gaugers went about their inspection, nothing was left to be found.

LANG STRANG

Provost Strang of Forfar had two sons, Robert and William, who emigrated to Sweden and became very successful merchants there. Wanting to give back to the town which had given them their start in life, they sent a large sum of money as a gift to the poor of the town, along with two silver bells which would chime sweetly in the church, bells which were given the names 'Six O'Clock' and 'Eight O'Clock'.

But as their fortunes grew, the Strang brothers wanted to give an even bigger gift to Forfar, and they hired the Swedish royal family's own metalsmith to create a much bigger, grander bell than any which graced a Scottish kirk at the time. This bell was made of brass, with a fine silver clapper, and it was four feet high and three feet wide. It was decorated all over with intricate patterns, and bore the Forfar coat of arms, as well as inscriptions with the Strang brothers' names.

By the time the smith had finished making the bell, Robert had died, so William was left to ensure it made its way safely home to Forfar. He entrusted it to the care of the ship *Grace of God* in Stockholm, which was bound for Dundee. The bell crossed the ocean safely, but trouble struck in Dundee. Jealous that their own city boasted no bell so grand, the harbour-men at Dundee tore out the silver clapper and cast it into the Tay. The town officials had to be bribed with a large payment to let the bell continue on its journey after it came off the ship.

But the bell made it to Forfar in the end, where it remains to this day, fondly known as Lang Strang. And a local smith by the name of David Falconer made a replacement clapper, which is still sounding clear and strong after hundreds of years.

THE STIRRUP CUP

On a quiet day in Forfar in 1670, a woman who kept an inn was busy brewing ale for her customers. As she always did, she set a cog of freshly brewed ale out by her doorstep, to allow the air to cool it to a more palatable temperature. As she went about her work in the house, the ale stood unwatched. Her neighbour's cow, loose and wandering past, felt a bit thirsty and spotted what looked like a lovely refreshing pot of water. After a few slurps, the cow got rather a taste for it and drank up every drop.

When the innkeeper came back to take her ale in, she was furious to find it gone! And it wasn't hard to spot the culprit, for the cow was staggering about all over the town, crashing through kailyards and washing lines with abandon. She stormed round to her neighbour's house and demanded compensation. But her neighbour said it was her own fault for leaving the drink unattended.

The innkeeper was not for letting it go. She took the matter to the authorities, and soon she faced her neighbour – as the cow was unable to represent herself – in the Forfar courthouse.

The judge was stumped. He'd never heard such a case in his life.

'If ony ither body took a drink in my ale-hoose they'd hae to pay for it!' insisted the innkeeper.

'Tell me,' the judge said to the neighbour. 'Was the cow standing when she took the drink?'

'Wis she standing! Tell me, man, hoo else wid a coo tak a drink?!'

'Well, if the drink was taken standing at the door of the ale-house, ancient custom holds that it was a stirrup cup, a deoch-an-doras offered in goodwill, and it would not be right to charge for it.'

The innkeeper was not pleased. But thanks to a drunken cow in Forfar, the custom of the stirrup cup was enshrined in Scots law, and the saying 'Be like the coo o Farfar – tak a standin drink!' was born.

The Sword of Deuchar

Deuchar of Deuchar was an ancient hero of Angus. He was a giant man, with six fingers on each hand and six toes on each foot, and his strength was ten times that of a normal man. In the year 1000, he fought and slew a ferocious wild boar at Coortford on the Noran Water, dealing the final blow with his trusty sword. The king was so impressed that he made Deuchar a gift of land near Fern, and that was where he made his home. Ten years later, Deuchar fought the Norse invaders at the Battle of Barry. Although he fought well and bravely, he was finally stabbed by an even taller and mightier Viking, and Deuchar was dead. His faithful servant, who had accompanied him into battle, knew his family would want to have his sword as a memorial, and to pass down to his sons when they grew. But when he tried to take it from Deuchar's dead hand, his grip was still so tight it could not be prised away. In the end, his servant had to chop his hand off to release the sword.

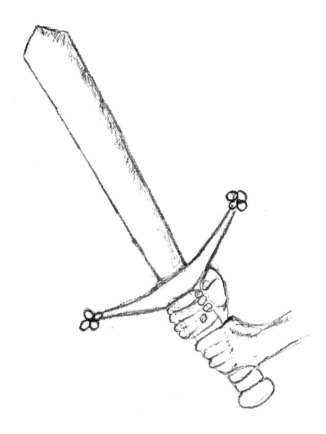

The sword which was brought home from the Battle of Barry was passed down through the Deuchar family for generations, and they used it to fight in the Scottish Wars of Independence. All the Deuchar men took after their ancestor's tall stature, so they could handle the huge weapon easily. But one Deuchar warrior lost a duel with the Laird of Ogil, and he took the sword for himself. Ogil had it shortened to fit his smaller size.

But a few generations later, the sword found its way back to the Deuchar family, and it is still in their possession today. Their family crest depicts a sword in hand and a boar's head, symbolising their ancestor's heroic achievements.

BALNABREICH DEN

Balnabreich Den, by the River South Esk between Brechin and Careston, was a popular spot for walkers and lovers of scenery. The only drawback was the ghost – a white wife who could never rest until she could share her terrible secret with a living soul. But she could never get close enough to anyone for long enough to accomplish this task, and a few of the old folk of Brechin had a good reason to keep her around. You see, she was thought of as a very useful ghost in some ways. She would often appear to young couples courting in the den who were on the verge of straying too late into the night. A waggle of her pale bony fingers sent many a pair of young lovers shrieking back into the safety of the town, terrified but with their honour remaining intact.

KING'S CADGER ROAD

Leading inland from Montrose, going towards Forfar, is an ancient right of way known as the King's Cadger Road. In the days when Forfar was home to the Scottish court, the finest fresh fish was sent down this road from Usan, and the bearer of the fish was to travel unmolested, by royal decree.

But on one occasion, when he was returning from Forfar with his pay in his pocket, the king's cadger was waylaid on the road by the Baron of Rossie and his son, who took his money and killed him. The king was furious when he discovered this and oversaw their trial and execution himself. The pair were sentenced to be hanged at the top of Kinnoul Hill near Rossie, and the scaffold was duly built. The condemned men were not resigned to their fate, and hesitated when the hangman told them to climb the steps up to the gallows. In a fury, the king rose and ordered them, 'Mount, boys!' This command was immortalised forever in the place name Mountboy, still seen in Mountboy Farm near the Moor of Rossie.

The more prosaic (and likely) explanation is that Mountboy comes from the French 'mont bois', a wooded mount.

Jock Tamson's Bairns

The fishing town of Usan, a little south of Montrose, lays a claim to the origin of a famous Scottish phrase. There was a thriving drinking den in the town, run by a John Thomson – known to all his friends and clientele, of which there were many, as Jock Tamson. Jock was a firm believer in practising what he preached, so he spent as much time pouring himself pints and joining in with the revelries as he did behind the bar running the pub. He did not believe in doing things by the book, either. He was more than happy to take a barrel of bargain whisky from a passing boat without asking too many questions about where it came from, and he certainly had not applied for a public house licence. And one night, when the songs and drams were in full flow, the customs officers paid a visit. They asked one of the drinkers to point out who ran the drinking establishment.

'Oh no, this is no public house,' replied the drinker. 'This is just a wee family gathering. Ye see, I'm a close relative of the host.'

So the officers moved on, and they asked another drinker, and another, and another. And each time, they got the same answer – everyone in that room said they were a close relation of the man of the house, so there was no pub operating at all, just a good old family sing-song.

'Am I expected to assume you are *all* part of the same family?' huffed one of the customs officers.

'Indeed we are,' came a cheery voice from beside the fireplace. 'We're a' Jock Tamson's bairns!'

Bibliography and Further Reading

Barrett, Dom Michael, *A Calendar of Scottish Saints* (Fort Augustus: Abbey Press, 1919)

Burke, J., *Dinnae Fleg the Bairns* (Dundee: Broken Windee Publishing, n.d.)

Cameron, David Kerr, *The Ballad and the Plough* (London: Futura, 1979)

Day, James Wentworth, *The Queen Mother's Family Story* (London: Robert Hale, 1979)

Edwards, David Herschell, *Around the Ancient City* (Brechin: Brechin Advertiser, 1887)

Edwards, David Herschell, *Historical Guide to Edzell and Glenesk Districts* (Brechin: Brechin Advertiser, 1893)

Fleming, Maurice, *The Sidlaws: Tales, Traditions and Ballads* (Edinburgh: Mercat Press, 2000)

Fraser, Duncan, *Glen of the Rowan Trees* (Montrose: Standard Press, 1974)

Fraser, Duncan, *The Flower People* (Montrose: Standard Press, 1977)

Gibson, Colin, *Folklore of Tayside* (Dundee: Dundee Art Galleries & Museums Service, 1959)

Guthrie, James Cargill, *The Vale of Strathmore: Its Scenes and Legends* (Edinburgh: William Paterson, 1875)

Inglis, W. Mason, *Annals of an Angus Parish* (Dundee: Leng & Co, 1888)

Jervise, Andrew, *The History and Traditions of the Land of the Lindsays* (Edinburgh: David Douglas, 1882)

Lowson, Alexander, *Tales, Traditions and Legends of Forfarshire* (Forfar: John Macdonald, 1891)

Lowson, Alexander, *John Guidfollow: A Romance of Forfarshire* (Glasgow: Thomas D. Morrison, 1890)

Mann, Ernest Simpson, *The Kirn Poke O Farfarshire – Facts and Folklore o the Coontie* (Forfar: Oliver McPherson, n.d.)

Marshall, William, *Historic Scenes in Forfarshire* (Edinburgh: William Oliphant & Co, 1875)

Martin, George M., *Dundee Worthies* (David Winter & Son: Dundee, 1934)

McHardy, Stuart, *Speakin O Dundee: Tales Telt Aroun the Toon* (Edinburgh: Luath, 2010)

Millar, Alexander Hastie, *Haunted Dundee* (Dundee: Malcolm C. Macleod, 1923)

Morris, Ruth and Frank Morris, *Scottish Healing Wells* (Sandy: Alethea Press, 1982)

Myles, James, *Rambles in Forfarshire* (Edinburgh: A&C Black, 1850)

O' Donnell, Elliott, *Scottish Ghost Stories* (London: Kegan Paul, 1911)

Reid, Alan, *The Royal Burgh of Forfar* (Forfar: Herald Office, 1902)

Stewart, Sheila, *Pilgrims of the Mist: The Stories of Scotland's Travelling People* (Edinburgh: Birlinn, 2008)

Taylor, Alex H., *Angus Lore and Legend* (Alex H. Taylor, 1988)

Warden, Alexander J., *Angus or Forfarshire: The Land and People, Descriptive and Historical* (Dundee: Charles Alexander & Co, 1880)

Whyte, Betsy, *The Yellow on the Broom* (Edinburgh: Chambers, 1979)

Whyte, Betsy, *Red Rowans and Wild Honey* (Edinburgh: Canongate, 1990)

Local newspapers throughout the nineteenth and twentieth centuries are also a rich source of folklore. D.H. Edwards wrote on folk tales as 'Auld Eppie' in the *Brechin Advertiser*; William Harvey and J.A. Rollo wrote antiquarian columns in the *Dundee Advertiser*, which give versions of many historical legends; and the Dundee and Angus editions of the *People's Journal* have included countless versions of local stories as articles, letters or poems over the years.

The School of Scottish Studies Archives are a major source for oral history and recorded stories. Many of their recordings can be listened to online on the website Tobar an Dualchas, at www.tobarandualchais.co.uk/en/. In particular, here I have included stories from Betsy Whyte (SA1979.004, her stories of Glamis), Jean Rodger's Forfar stories and rhymes (SA1976.078) and Stanley Robertson's story of the Banshee of Glenisla (SA1979.022).